Revenge of the G

CH

The trail stretched out endlessly ahead, a ribbon of dry earth cutting through the vast emptiness of the frontier. The horizon wavered in the heat, the land around it baked into shades of ochre and brown under the relentless sun. Nash rode in silence, the steady plod of his mare's hooves the only sound to break the stillness. The air was heavy, pressing down like a weight, but it was the weight inside him that bore down hardest.

Emily's face flickered in his mind, unbidden but ever-present. He could still see her smile, the way her laughter softened the hard edges of life on the ranch. But the memory twisted like a blade, replaced by the hollow ache of her absence. Nash shifted in the saddle, his jaw tightening as he forced the thought away. *Keep moving,* he told himself. *There's nothing behind worth holding onto.*

The ranch was gone to him now. Not in the literal sense—it still stood, the land still tilled, the cattle still grazed. But it wasn't his anymore. Emily had been its heart, and with her gone, the place was a ghost of what it once was. He'd buried her there, alongside the child they'd never get to know. The grief had been too much to bear, and so he'd left, seeking solace in the endless trail.

Wyatt Steele

But solace wasn't what he'd found.

Nash adjusted the brim of his hat, his eyes scanning the horizon. The land was empty, as it often was, the stillness almost oppressive. Yet it suited him—this hollow, endless expanse. No ties, no faces to remember, no graves to tend.

The sound of voices broke the quiet, distant but sharp enough to carry on the dry breeze. Nash pulled his mare to a stop, his hand instinctively brushing against the worn handle of his Colt. He turned his head toward the sound, his keen eyes narrowing. A group of figures moved ahead, clustered near a scraggly line of mesquite trees.

It didn't take long to see what was happening. A young boy, no older than ten, stood frozen in fear, his arms raised defensively as two rough-looking men loomed over him. One of the men—a wiry figure with a jagged scar across his cheek—shoved the boy backward, sending him sprawling into the dirt.

"Come on, kid," the man sneered. "You got somethin' worth takin', or you just wastin' our time?"

The boy scrambled to his feet, clutching a small bundle to his chest. "I ain't got nothin'," he stammered, his voice trembling. "Please, just leave me be!"

The second man laughed, a low, cruel sound that set Nash's teeth on edge. "We'll be the judge of that."

The Revenge of The Gunfighter

First published in eBook and paperback 2024

© Wyatt Steele

The right of Wyatt Steele to be identified as the author of this work has been asserted by her in accordance with the Copyright, Designs and Patents Act 1988.

All rights reserved. No part of this publication may be reproduced, stored in or introduced into a retrieval system, or transmitted, in any form, or by any means (electronic, mechanical, photocopying, recording or otherwise) without the prior written permission of the writer. Any person who does any unauthorized act in relation to this publication may be liable to criminal prosecution and civil claims for damages.

Thank you for respecting the hard work of this author.

Wyatt Steele

Contents

CHAPTER ONE	3
CHAPTER TWO	7
CHAPTER THREE	21
CHAPTER FOUR	35
CHAPTER FIVE	46
CHAPTER SIX	61
CHAPTER SEVEN	71
CHAPTER EIGHT	79
CHAPTER NINE	88
CHAPTER TEN	105
CHAPTER ELEVEN	115
CHAPTER TWELVE	123
CHAPTER THIRTEEN	137
CHAPTER FOURTEEN	153
EPILOGUE	172

Nash sat motionless in the saddle for a moment, weighing his options. He didn't want to get involved. Trouble had a way of sticking to a man, and he'd spent the better part of his life trying to shake it loose. But as the scarred man grabbed the boy by the collar, shaking him like a rag doll, Nash felt a spark of something long buried stir to life.

"Damn it," he muttered under his breath.

He urged his mare forward, the soft thud of hooves catching the men's attention. The boy's wide, terrified eyes darted toward Nash, and for a fleeting moment, hope flickered in his expression.

"Morning, boys," Nash said, his tone calm but carrying an edge of steel. He stopped his horse a few paces away, his hand resting casually on the Colt at his hip. "Looks like you're pickin' on someone who can't fight back. That doesn't sit too well with me."

The scarred man turned, his lip curling in disdain. "And who the hell are you, cowboy? This ain't your business."

"Maybe not," Nash replied, his voice as steady as the horizon behind him. "But it's my trail, and you're in the way."

The second man, stockier and armed with a rifle slung over his shoulder, took a step forward. "You got a death wish, stranger?"

"Nope," Nash replied.

The man grinned, and then his hand dropped to his piece.

Nash's hand moved in a blur, the Colt clearing leather before the stocky man had his revolver half-way from its holster. The sharp crack of gunfire split the air, and the man cried out, clutching his thigh as he crumpled to the ground.

The scarred man froze, his eyes flicking between Nash and his injured partner. Nash leveled the Colt at him, the barrel steady as a judge's gavel.

"You've got two choices," he said evenly. "Walk away now, or end up like him. Your call."

The man hesitated, his jaw clenching, but the cold finality in Nash's gaze left little room for argument. He spat on the ground and backed away, dragging his injured companion with him. "This ain't over," he growled, his voice laced with venom. "You'll regret this, cowboy."

Nash watched them go, his revolver still raised until they disappeared into the distance. Only then did he holster it, exhaling slowly. He turned his attention to the boy, who was still crouched in the dirt, clutching his bundle tightly.

"You alright, kid?" Nash asked, his tone softer now.

The boy nodded shakily, his eyes wide with awe and fear. "Thank you," he said, his voice barely audible.

Nash swung down from his horse, kneeling to meet the boy's gaze. "Don't thank me," he said gruffly. "Just stay outta trouble. The world's got enough of it without you addin' more."

The boy looked like he wanted to say something else, but Nash was already climbing back into the saddle. He tipped his hat and urged his mare forward, leaving the boy and his gratitude behind.

As the trail stretched out before him once more, Nash felt no sense of satisfaction. The scarred man's parting words hung in his mind like a storm cloud. Trouble had a way of finding him, and now it was coming. But as always, he kept moving.

CHAPTER TWO

The sun hung low in the sky as Nash rode into Blackrock, its dying light casting long shadows over the battered town. Dust clung to the air, stirred by the restless movements of horses and wagons that seemed to linger at the edges of the main street. Blackrock wasn't much—a cluster of weathered buildings and sagging storefronts lining a single thoroughfare framed by the distant, jagged peaks of the canyons.

Nash's mare plodded wearily through the dirt, her gait slowing as they passed a blacksmith's shop where the forge glowed faintly. A handful of locals stood nearby, their conversations quiet, their eyes darting toward the saloon at the end of the street. A sign swung lazily in the breeze above it, the paint faded but still legible: *Sadie's Place.*

Nash dismounted, tying his mare to the hitching rail outside the saloon. The air here felt heavier, the kind of weight that came with fear, with people too afraid to speak their minds. His gaze swept over the street as he adjusted his hat, catching sight of a cluster of men lounging near the general store. They were rough-looking, with the kind of swagger that came from knowing they could act with impunity.

Revenge of the Gunfighter

This place stinks of trouble, Nash thought as he stepped into the saloon.

The saloon was dimly lit, the air thick with the smell of stale beer and cheap tobacco. A piano sat unused in the corner, its keys yellowed with age. A handful of patrons occupied the tables, nursing drinks and casting furtive glances toward the bar, where a woman poured whiskey with practiced efficiency.

The woman behind the bar had a presence that demanded attention. Her auburn hair was swept back in a loose tie, strands falling just enough to soften the sharpness of her expression. Her eyes, sharp and unyielding, scanned the room with the practiced vigilance of someone who'd seen trouble more times than she cared to count. She moved with purpose, her hands steady as she set a glass on the counter, the gesture more a warning than a welcome.

Nash approached the bar, his boots scuffing softly against the worn floorboards. Her gaze snapped to him, hawk-like and assessing, her lips pulling into the faintest hint of a smirk—not friendly, but not entirely hostile either.

"New face," she said, her voice low and edged with suspicion. She didn't bother with pleasantries. "Don't get many of those 'round here."

"Just passin' through," Nash replied, his tone measured, his eyes meeting hers without flinching.

She tilted her head, studying him with the air of someone weighing a gamble. "Is that so?" Her hand gestured vaguely toward a shotgun resting on a ledge just behind the bar, within easy reach. "Long as you're just passin' through, we won't have a problem. But if trouble comes knocking, I'm not shy about handling it. This is my place and I like to keep it peaceful."

Nash's lips twitched, almost forming a smile. It wasn't the warmest welcome he'd ever received in a saloon—in fact, it might have been the coldest. Still, there was something almost amusing about her bluntness.

"I'll keep that in mind," he said dryly, leaning slightly against the bar, then added, "So you'll be Sadie."

The woman nodded, sharp eyes narrowed, catching the flicker of amusement in his tone. "Something funny about that, mister?"

Sadie arched a brow, skepticism etched across her sharp features, and without waiting for an invitation, she grabbed a bottle of whiskey from the shelf behind her and poured a measured shot into a glass. Instead of sliding it across the bar, she kept her hand firmly on it, her fingers curling around the glass like it might try to escape.

"This is a two-bit saloon," she said evenly, her tone hard. "We don't do credit, and we don't pour for free."

Nash met her gaze without flinching, the faintest flicker of amusement tugging at the corner of his mouth. He didn't argue, didn't try to charm her. Instead, he dug two coins out of his pocket and slid them across the counter with deliberate care. They stopped just short of her fingers.

Sadie eyed the coins like a hawk studying prey, then picked them up and examined each one as if she expected them to be counterfeit. Only after she was satisfied did she push the glass toward him with a curt nod.

Nash wrapped his fingers around the drink, lifting it slowly to his lips. "Seems like a fine place to me," he said, his tone as dry as the desert wind.

Sadie let out a quiet huff, crossing her arms. "You'll change your tune soon enough," Sadie leaned forward, lowering her voice. "The kind where you either keep your head down or Kade's boys put it on a spike."

Then Nash slid the empty glass back across the bar, the soft scrape of glass against wood cutting through the quiet hum of the saloon. He reached into his pocket again, fishing out two more coins. After a brief hesitation, he added a third and pushed them toward the woman with the same deliberate care as before.

"Another," he said evenly, his voice polite but firm. "If you don't mind, ma'am."

Sadie paused her wiping, her sharp eyes locking onto his like she was trying to read the measure of the man before her. For a moment, he thought she might refuse or toss some cutting remark his way. Instead, she gave a small, almost imperceptible nod. Without a word, she turned to the shelf behind her, bypassing the bottle she'd poured from earlier.

From beneath the bar, she retrieved a different bottle. This one was darker, the label worn and faded, and the glass was thick with age. It was a whiskey for those who knew the difference. She poured him a generous measure, then slid the glass back across the counter with a little more care than she had the first.

Nash picked up the glass and raised it slightly in a quiet gesture of thanks before taking a sip. The difference was immediate. The whiskey was smoother and richer, with a warmth that lingered in his chest instead of clawing at his throat. He let it settle for a moment before speaking.

"Much obliged," he said, his tone carrying a trace of genuine appreciation. "That's more like it."

Sadie leaned on the bar, her gaze still wary but with a flicker of something softer. "Don't expect it every time," she said, her voice still sharp but without the earlier edge. "You pay for what you get, and most folks around here don't bother reaching that deep in their pockets."

Nash chuckled faintly, the sound low and rough. "Most folks don't know what they're missing."

Sadie arched a brow, her lips curving into the ghost of a smirk. "Maybe. Or maybe most folks know better than to expect something that doesn't last."

Nash didn't reply. He took another sip, savoring the quiet moment, knowing full well that nothing good ever did last—but for now, this was enough.

Sadie leaned back slightly, crossing her arms as she regarded Nash with that hawk-like gaze. "This town," she said, her voice low and steady, "is owned by Elijah Kade."

The name hung in the air like a storm cloud, heavy and ominous. Nash didn't react right away, but his grip on the glass tightened slightly. He took another slow sip, letting the whiskey burn its way down as he waited for her to continue.

"If you've got any sense," Sadie went on, her tone edged with something between warning and resignation, "you'll finish that drink, saddle up, and keep riding. Because Kade doesn't take kindly to strangers."

Nash set the glass down carefully, his expression unreadable. "Elijah Kade," he repeated, his voice as calm as the surface of a still pond. "Don't reckon I've heard that name before."

Sadie let out a quiet huff, her skepticism plain. "You're not from around here, so I'll give you the benefit of the doubt. Kade runs the mines in Blackrock. He's got men everywhere, and every one of 'em's meaner than the last. This place is his, and anyone who forgets it usually doesn't last long."

Nash ran a finger along the rim of his glass, his gaze drifting toward the shotgun still resting on the ledge behind her. "Sounds like a man who doesn't leave much room for negotiation."

"He doesn't," Sadie said bluntly. "And he won't hesitate to make an example out of anyone who tries. I've seen it happen. So if you've got any sense, cowboy, you'll finish what's left of your drink and ride out before Kade even knows you're here."

Nash met her gaze, his expression as unreadable as ever. He picked up the glass, turning it slightly in his hand before taking another sip. The whiskey was smooth, but there was a bitter edge to the moment that the drink couldn't dull.

Nash's fingers traced the rim of the glass before he set it down deliberately, his movements slow and measured. "Appreciate the advice," he said at last, his tone calm. But beneath the surface of his words lay a weight—a quiet defiance that lingered in the air between them.

Sadie's sharp eyes narrowed, her expression hardening as she studied him. She leaned forward slightly, resting her palms on the bar. "Somehow, I don't think you're the type to take it," she said, her voice low and edged with something like resignation.

Without a word, Nash slid the glass back toward her. Three coins followed, their metallic clink breaking the silence. Sadie's gaze flicked to the coins, then back to Nash. She huffed softly, shaking her head as she reached for the bottle. The whiskey poured in a steady stream, catching the light before she slid the glass back to him.

Nash lifted the refilled glass but didn't take a drink, his sharp eyes scanning the saloon, as though weighing the room for threats. The faint creak of the swinging doors drew his attention, and he turned slightly, his posture tightening.

Two men stepped into the saloon, their boots striking the floor with slow, deliberate purpose. Dust kicked up at their heels as they moved, and the air in the room seemed to shift. They were big, broad-shouldered brutes with hard, weathered faces—the kind of men who carried the weight of violence like a second skin. Their presence alone was enough to make the other patrons shrink back into their seats, heads lowering to avoid drawing attention.

The man on the left had a jagged scar slicing across his forehead, the pale, puckered skin catching the dim light of the saloon. His eyes were dark, sharp, and predatory as they scanned the room. His companion, equally imposing, carried a sense of quiet menace, his hands resting loosely at his sides, not far from the revolver on his hip.

The scarred man's gaze locked onto a young man sitting at a table near the back of the saloon. The boy was barely more than a sixteen

Nash reckoned, his clothes worn and patched, his face pale as he stared down at his empty plate, trying to disappear into the shadows.

"Turner," the scarred man barked, his voice cutting through the room like a whip crack. The young man flinched, his head jerking up as if he'd been struck. "You've been late with your quota. Kade don't like that."

The room went still. The faint clink of glasses and low murmur of conversation had vanished, replaced by a tense, suffocating silence. All eyes darted toward the scarred man and his companion, though no one dared to linger for too long.

At the bar, Nash watched, his glass hovering near his lips but untouched. His eyes narrowed slightly as he studied the two men, his jaw tightening imperceptibly. Next to him, Sadie muttered under her breath, something low and bitter, as she reached for the shotgun resting on the ledge behind her.

Nash set his glass down quietly, his hand brushing against the Colt on his hip. He didn't move, didn't speak, but the faint shift in his posture said everything. Trouble had walked into the saloon, and it was only a matter of time before it found its mark.

The young man—barely more than a boy—stood slowly, his shoulders squared but his hands trembling. Caleb Turner had the lean build of someone who worked hard but never quite got enough to eat. His blue eyes burned with defiance as he faced the two men.

"I ain't payin' anymore," Caleb said, his voice shaking but resolute. "The miners don't owe Kade a damn thing."

The scarred man laughed, a harsh, humorless sound. "You hear that, boys? The kid thinks he's got a backbone."

He stepped forward, grabbing Caleb by the front of his shirt and yanking him closer. "You're gonna pay, Turner. One way or another." Nash's jaw clenched as the tension in the room grew thick enough to choke. His gut told him to stay out of it. This wasn't his fight, and stepping in would only paint a target squarely on his back. But when the second man grabbed Caleb by the shirt and yanked him to his feet, raising a fist with every intention of striking him, something inside Nash twisted like a blade.

The saloon's oppressive silence pressed down harder, and then it snapped.
"Let him go," Nash said, his voice low but sharp, cutting through the air like a crack of thunder.

Every head in the room turned toward him. The scarred man froze, his fist still cocked mid-swing. His sneer faltered as he slowly released Caleb, shoving the young miner back into his chair. Turning, he sized up Nash with a look of disdain, his lip curling like a cornered dog baring its teeth.

Wyatt Steele

"Who the hell are you?" the scarred man demanded, his voice a growl.

"Just a man who doesn't like bullies," Nash replied evenly. His tone was calm, but there was steel beneath it, a quiet promise of violence.

The second man, broader and meaner, let out a low chuckle that didn't reach his cold eyes. "You picked the wrong town to play hero," he sneered. "You think one man's gonna scare us?"

His hand dropped toward the revolver at his side, but Nash moved before anyone could even draw a breath. The Colt was out in a flash, its barrel gleaming under the weak saloon lights, pointed squarely at the broad man's chest. The sudden motion sent a ripple of gasps through the room, the weight of the moment crashing down like an anvil.

"You sure you want to do this?" Nash asked, his voice steady as a rock. "I've got nothing to lose, but you've got a lot to bleed."

The scarred man froze, his hand hovering inches from his own holster. The smirk that had been playing on his lips melted away, replaced by something harder—uncertainty, and beneath it, a flicker of fear. Nash's expression didn't change, his eyes locked onto the man's like a hawk watching its prey stumble.

The broad man licked his lips, his bravado wavering. Nash didn't flinch, the Colt as steady as if it were an extension of his own arm. The room

held its collective breath, the tension threatening to snap like a coiled spring.
Finally, the scarred man raised both hands slowly, his lip curling in frustration. "This ain't over," he spat, jerking his head toward the door. "Come on."

His partner glared at Nash, his face twisted with anger, but he didn't make a move. The two of them stormed out, the doors swinging shut behind them with a loud crack.

The silence that followed was deafening. For a long beat, no one moved. Then, slowly, the saloon began to stir, the patrons returning to their drinks with nervous glances, doing their best to pretend they hadn't seen anything.

Caleb stumbled to his feet, his face pale but his eyes wide with a mix of gratitude and awe. "Thank you," he stammered, his voice trembling. "I didn't think—"

"Don't thank me," Nash cut him off, sliding his Colt back into its holster with a practiced motion. His tone was cold, almost dismissive. "I didn't do it for you."

Without another word, he turned back to the bar, lifting his glass and downing the rest of his whiskey in one smooth motion. The burn in his throat was nothing compared to the fire still simmering inside him.

Sadie, who had been watching from behind the bar, leaned forward, her expression unreadable but her voice quiet and sharp. "You've made yourself a target."

Nash shrugged, setting the empty glass down and placing a coin beside it. "Wouldn't be the first time," he said, his tone flat.

Sadie hesitated, her sharp eyes fixed on Nash as if weighing some invisible scale. For a moment, the only sound in the saloon was the low murmur of the patrons trying to act like they hadn't just witnessed a standoff. Then, finally, she spoke.

"I've got rooms for rent upstairs," she said, her voice steady but carrying a hint of something unspoken. "Two bits if you want one."

Nash glanced at her, his expression unreadable. He didn't move right away, letting her offer hang in the air. "Not sure that's the wisest idea," he said quietly, his voice low enough not to carry beyond the bar. "Not after I just drew down on Kade's boys. Renting me a room might put you square in their sights."

Sadie's lips pressed into a thin line, her gaze hardening. "Maybe it's time someone stirred the pot," she said flatly. "Life's been getting a little too boring around here anyway."

Nash studied her for a long moment, his own sharp gaze meeting hers. There was something in her tone that struck a chord—defiance, maybe, or just the kind of reckless courage that came from being pushed too far. He reached into his pocket, pulled out two more coins, and slid them across the bar.

"Fair enough," he said. "I'll take the room."

Sadie picked up the coins and tucked them away without a word. Then she nodded toward the staircase at the far end of the saloon. "Second door on the left. Lock works, but I wouldn't count on it keeping anyone out who really wants in."

"I wouldn't expect it to," Nash replied, tipping his hat slightly. He picked up his saddlebags from the floor and slung them over his shoulder, his movements calm and deliberate.

As he made his way toward the stairs, Sadie called after him, her tone laced with dry humor. "Don't get too comfortable. Around here, we don't get many happy endings."

Nash paused at the base of the staircase, glancing back at her. "Never expected one," he said simply before disappearing up the steps.

Blackrock wasn't just dangerous anymore—it was a powder keg, and he'd just lit the fuse.

CHAPTER THREE

Wyatt Steele

Nash woke to the first gray light of dawn filtering through a cracked, uneven windowpane. The room was small, barely more than a box, with walls that leaned slightly inward as though the building itself had grown tired of holding its shape. Dust motes hung in the dim light, swirling lazily in the still air.

The bed beneath him creaked with every shift of his weight, its mattress thin and lumpy, stuffed with something that felt more like old straw than feathers. A threadbare quilt was draped haphazardly over him, its edges frayed from years of wear. The pillow smelled faintly of stale whiskey and smoke, the kind of scent that never left a place like this.

His saddlebags rested on a rickety wooden chair in the corner, next to his boots and hat. The chair leaned awkwardly to one side, one of its legs slightly shorter than the others, and Nash figured it was a miracle it hadn't collapsed under the weight. On a small table by the bed, his Colt sat within easy reach, the metal gleaming faintly in the pale light. Beside it, a half-burned candle sat in a saucer, the wax hardened into jagged drips.

The room had the distinct feel of temporary existence—functional but devoid of comfort. The wallpaper, once patterned with faded florals, now hung in curling strips where moisture had seeped through the cracks. A single wooden peg on the wall served as a coat hook, but it was empty save for a spider web stretching across the top corner.

From downstairs, the faint murmur of voices and the clink of glass broke the early morning stillness. The saloon was waking up, and with it, the town of Blackrock. Nash rubbed his eyes, the weight of the previous night still heavy on his shoulders. He swung his legs over the side of the bed, the floorboards creaking beneath him as he stood.

It wasn't much, this room. But it was enough for now.

Outside, Blackrock was already alive with the sounds of its routine misery. The clang of hammers at the blacksmith's forge, the groan of wagon wheels rolling over rutted dirt, and the occasional bark of laughter from Kade's men patrolling the street. Nash sat at a corner table in Sadie's Place, a cup of coffee cooling in his hands as he watched the town through the grimy saloon window.

Sadie walked up and set a plate of biscuits and bacon in front of him. "Figured you'd want something solid before you hit the trail," she said, her tone brisk but not unkind.

Nash didn't answer right away, his eyes fixed on a group of miners trudging by outside. Their faces were hollowed by hunger and exhaustion, their clothes patched and dusty. They moved like shadows, avoiding eye contact with anyone who might take too much notice of them.

"Kade's doing?" Nash asked finally, his voice low.

Sadie leaned against the table, crossing her arms. "He's been bleeding them dry for years," she said. "Started with small fees—protection, he called it. Then, it was a cut of the gold. Now he owns them, body and soul."

Nash took a sip of his coffee, his gaze unwavering. "And nobody's done anything about it?"

Sadie gave a humorless laugh. "You think anyone around here's got the firepower to stand up to him? He's got thirty men, all meaner than rattlesnakes. Anyone who tries to fight back ends up buried out in the canyon."

Sadie shook her head, her expression tight with frustration as she reached across the table to collect Nash's empty plate. The scrape of porcelain against the wood broke the silence between them as she tucked it under one arm and wiped the table down with a damp cloth, her movements brisk and efficient.

"You want anything else?" she asked, her voice steady but distant, as though she was already preparing herself for the next round of disappointment this town seemed to breed.

Nash leaned back slightly in his chair, his fingers still curled around the warm mug of coffee. He glanced down at it, then back up at her. "Another cup, if you've got it," he said. "It's good. Wouldn't mind one more."

Revenge of the Gunfighter

Sadie paused, the faintest flicker of surprise crossing her face. She hadn't been expecting that, but before she could stop herself, the corners of her mouth tugged upward in a reluctant, fleeting smile. It was there and gone in an instant, like the first crack of sunlight after a storm.

"Coming right up," she muttered, turning on her heel and heading toward the bar.

Nash watched her go, his expression unreadable, though there was a flicker of something in his eyes—amusement, maybe, or a quiet understanding. He took another sip of the coffee he had left, savoring the moment of warmth in a place that seemed so cold.

Sadie returned a moment later with a fresh cup, setting it down in front of him with the same efficiency as before. "There," she said, her tone edging toward gruff, though she didn't meet his eyes. "Enjoy."

Nash tipped his hat slightly in thanks, lifting the fresh cup to his lips. The coffee was hot, smooth, and stronger than he'd expected—a pleasant surprise in a place like Blackrock. He set the mug down carefully, his gaze settling on Sadie as she wiped down the counter.

"Why don't you join me?" he said, his tone casual but carrying just enough weight to make her pause.

Sadie froze mid-wipe, her sharp eyes flicking to him, suspicion flashing across her face like a reflex. "I've got work to do," she replied briskly, though there was a faint hesitation in her voice.

"Doesn't look like much of a rush," Nash said, gesturing toward the nearly empty saloon with a faint tilt of his head. His voice was calm, almost conversational, but there was something in the way he spoke that made it clear he wouldn't mind her company. "Sit. Have a cup yourself. Might be the only break you get all day."

Sadie hesitated, her grip tightening on the cloth in her hand. She glanced around the room, her eyes landing briefly on the shotgun still resting behind the bar before she sighed quietly. Tossing the cloth onto the counter, she grabbed a mug from the shelf and filled it from the pot. She walked over to the table with deliberate steps and pulled out a chair, the legs scraping softly against the floor as she sat down across from him.

"For the record," she said, her tone firm as she leaned back slightly in the chair, "I don't usually drink coffee with strangers."

Nash's lips twitched, the ghost of a smile playing at the corners of his mouth. "Don't worry. I won't take it personally."

Sadie took a sip of her coffee, studying him over the rim of her mug. "What's your angle, cowboy? You're not like most folks who pass through here."

"No angle," Nash replied, his voice even. "Just figured you might want to sit for a spell. This town doesn't seem like the kind of place that lets you do that often."

Sadie snorted softly, though there wasn't much humor in it. "You've got that right."

They sat in silence for a moment, the hum of the saloon settling around them. Nash didn't press her to speak, letting the quiet fill the space between them. It was Sadie who finally broke it, her voice softer now, but still laced with caution.

"So, cowboy," she said, her eyes narrowing slightly. "What are you really doing in Blackrock?"

Nash took another sip of his coffee, his gaze steady as he met hers. "Haven't quite figured that out yet," he admitted, his tone honest but guarded. "But I don't plan on staying long."

Sadie nodded slowly, though her expression suggested she wasn't entirely convinced. "Well," she said, leaning back in her chair, "if you're smart, you'll stick to that plan. This place has a way of chewing people up and spitting them out."

"Tell me about Kade," Nash said, his voice low.
Sadie glanced at him, her expression darkening. "You don't know him?"

"Nope, your Kade ain't as notorious as he'd like to think," Nash said. "Don't know the name."

"Let me guess," Nash said. "The miners traded one tyrant for another."

Wyatt Steele

Sadie nodded. "Now he owns the town. The mines, the stores, even the sheriff. Everyone pays him tribute, or they don't last long." Her sharp eyes softened, just for a moment, as if the memory carried a weight she hadn't shared in a long time. "Elijah Kade wasn't always like this," she said, her voice quieter now, tinged with something between regret and bitterness. "He came here almost ten years ago, back when Blackrock still had a little hope left. Back then, he was a preacher."

Nash raised an eyebrow, skepticism flickering in his gaze. "A preacher?"

Sadie nodded, leaning forward, her elbows on the bar. "Called himself a man of God. He said he was here to save souls and help the miners find faith. And for a while, folks believed him. He had a way about him, you know? The kind of voice that made you sit up and listen. He'd stand up there in that little church, talking about redemption, community, and how we could all make this town better if we just stuck together."

Nash sipped his coffee, his eyes narrowing. "Sounds like a good man. What happened?"

Sadie's laugh was short and humorless. "The mine happened. Biggest collapse Blackrock ever saw. Fifty men trapped underground, their families gathered outside, praying for a miracle. And Kade... he didn't just stand there and preach. He was one of the first to climb down into that pit,

digging with his bare hands, pulling men out one by one. He saved lives that day. A lot of 'em."
Nash tilted his head, waiting for the rest. He knew it was coming.

Sadie's voice grew colder, her gaze drifting to the far wall as if she could still see the shadows of what had been. "But then he found out the truth. The mine owner—Henry Carver, fat cur with more money than sense—had known the shaft was unstable. But he pushed the men to work it anyway. All for one last vein of gold. He knew it could collapse, and he didn't care."

Nash's expression hardened a flicker of understanding crossing his face. "Kade confronted him?"

Sadie's lips twisted into a bitter smile. "Oh, he did. Right there in front of half the town. He told Carver he had blood on his hands, and that the miners deserved justice. You know what Carver did? Laughed. Called him a fool for thinkin' anything could change. Said the miners were nothing but tools to be used up and thrown away."

She paused, her voice dropping to a near-whisper. "Kade snapped. Right there, in front of God and everyone, he shot Carver dead. One shot, clean between the eyes. The man didn't even have time to blink."

Nash exhaled slowly, leaning back in his chair. "And that was the end of Preacher Kade."

Wyatt Steele

Sadie nodded, her expression darkening. "He left town that night, disappeared for a week. When he came back, he wasn't a preacher anymore. He had a dozen men with him—armed to the teeth—and a new idea about how the world should work. If the miners couldn't have justice, he said, they'd take power instead."

"At first," Sadie continued, her voice growing sharper, "folks thought he was still on their side. He went after the mine owners, the land speculators, anyone who profited while the rest of us scraped by. Burned down their offices, ran them out of town, sometimes worse. People cheered him on, thought he was some kind of avenging angel. But it didn't take long for him to turn."

Nash's gaze narrowed. "Turned, how?"

Sadie's jaw tightened, her hands gripping the edge of the bar. "It stopped being about justice. He started taking what he wanted—land, money, people. Said it was payment for the miners, but the miners never saw a damn dollar of it. He surrounded himself with killers, men just as mean as he was. They'd beat anyone who got in their way, burn down homes, drag men out into the desert and leave 'em for the vultures."

Her voice dropped, filled with something colder now. "It's like the devil climbed into him the day he shot Carver and never let go. He doesn't just kill—he makes it a spectacle. Leaves bodies out where folks can see 'em, to remind us who's in charge. He keeps us all afraid, just enough to stop us from fighting back."

Nash didn't flinch under her stare. Instead, he picked up his coffee and took another slow sip, his expression unreadable. But something flickered in his eyes—something that might have been anger, or maybe just the recognition of a man who'd seen evil before and knew exactly what it looked like.

The saloon doors creaked and the sheriff stepped inside, his badge dull on his vest, his heavy boots scuffing against the worn wooden floor. He was a large man gone soft, his belly stretching the fabric of his dusty coat, his once-proud shoulders slumped under the weight of defeat. His bloodshot eyes scanned the room, landing on Sadie and then sliding to Nash, seated next to her, nursing his second cup of coffee.

"Sadie," Hayes greeted, his voice gravelly and weary. He tugged off his hat and slapped it against his leg, sending a cloud of dust into the air. "Didn't figure you'd still be open after that ruckus last night."

Sadie didn't look up. "What do you want, Amos?"

The sheriff's gaze flicked back to Nash, sizing him up with the practiced eye of a man who'd seen plenty of drifters come and go. "This him?" he asked, jerking his thumb toward Nash. "The one who thought it'd be smart to pull a gun on Kade's men?"

Sadie finally looked up, her expression sharp. "That's right. And he's probably done more for this town in one night than you've managed in the past year."

Hayes snorted, crossing the room with a heavy step. He stopped in front of Nash, his bulk casting a shadow over the drifter. "Another damn fool drifter," he muttered. "You think you're gonna roll in here and fix things? Take Kade down with that big iron on your hip?"

Nash's eyes met the sheriff's, calm but cold. He didn't move, didn't flinch, just took a deliberate sip of his coffee before setting the cup down. "I'm not here to fix your problems, Sheriff," he said evenly. "And I sure as hell don't plan to fight your battles for you."

"Good," Hayes barked, his lip curling. "'Cause this town don't need a hero. It needs a miracle."

Sadie slammed her hand down on the table, and stood. "The miners are barely hanging on, Amos. They're starving, scared, and tired. If someone doesn't stand up to Kade soon, this whole town's gonna collapse."

"And you think I don't know that?" Hayes growled, turning on her. His voice rose, anger flaring through the exhaustion. "What do you expect me to do, Sadie? I've got no deputies and a tin star that means Jake shit against thirty men armed to the teeth. Kade's got Blackrock by the throat, and he knows it."

Sadie stood, her hands clenched into fists at her sides. "You're the sheriff. That badge used to stand for something, but now you sit in that office, drinking yourself into a stupor while Kade tears this place apart. If you can't protect the people, then what the hell are you good for?"

Hayes' face darkened, his shoulders slumping further as her words hit home. For a moment, the only sound in the saloon was the distant clink of glasses and the shuffle of boots from the few patrons who pretended not to be listening.

Nash watched it all with the same unreadable expression, his fingers idly tracing the rim of his coffee cup. When the silence stretched too long, he stood, the scrape of his chair against the floor breaking the tension.

"You're wasting your breath, lady," he said, tipping his hat to Sadie before turning toward the door. "Some fights aren't worth the trouble."

Sadie stared after him, her jaw tightening as she bit back a retort. Hayes watched him go too, but the sheriff's face held something else— resentment, sure, but also shame, buried deep beneath the weariness of a man who'd long since stopped believing he could make a difference.

As the saloon doors swung shut behind Nash, the weight of Blackrock seemed to settle over everyone left inside, pressing harder with every breath.

Wyatt Steele

CHAPTER FOUR

Outside the sheriff's office, Caleb was waiting for Nash, his face pale but determined. He fell into step beside Nash as they walked down the street.

"You saw the sheriff," Caleb said, his voice tight. "He's not gonna do anything. That's why we need someone like you."

Nash glanced at him. "Like me?"

"Someone who can fight," Caleb said. "Someone who isn't afraid of Kade."

Nash stopped, turning to face the younger man. "Listen, kid. I've seen men like Kade before. They don't play fair, and they don't stop until they've taken everything. Hope doesn't win battles— bullets do. And Kade's got a hell of a lot more of those than you do."

Caleb's jaw clenched. "So what, we're just supposed to roll over? Let him take everything?"

"I didn't say that," Nash replied evenly. "But you'd better think long and hard about what you're willing to lose before you start something you can't finish."

Caleb stared at him, his fists clenched at his sides. "You're just like everyone else," he said bitterly. "Too scared to stand up."

Wyatt Steele

Nash didn't respond, his expression hard as stone. He turned and walked away, leaving Caleb standing alone in the street.

That evening, Nash sat on the porch of Sadie's Place, watching as the miners gathered near the general store. Their faces were a mosaic of weariness and anger, their voices hushed as they whispered among themselves. They looked toward the saloon occasionally, their eyes lingering on Nash like he was some kind of answer to their prayers.

Sadie joined him, her arms crossed as she leaned against the railing. "They're lookin' to you," she said quietly.

"They shouldn't," Nash replied. "I'm not here to save them."

"Maybe not," Sadie said, her tone sharp. "But you've stood your ground against Kade's men. And that's more than most folks in this town can say."

Nash didn't answer. He watched as Caleb approached the group, his voice rising above the murmurs as he tried to rally the miners. There was fire in the boy's words, but it was clear he was fighting an uphill battle. The men were scared, their spirits crushed under the weight of Kade's tyranny.

Sadie sighed, her gaze distant. "This town used to be something," she said. "Hard-working folks, decent lives. Then Kade came, and it all went to hell. Now we're just waiting for someone to make the first move."

Nash leaned back, his eyes on the darkening sky. "The first move's the easy part," he said quietly. "It's what comes after that'll kill you."

Sadie looked at him, her expression unreadable. "And you'd know all about that, wouldn't you?"

Nash didn't respond, but the weight of her words lingered as the night settled over Blackrock. The miners dispersed, their heads low, their hope dim. And Nash sat in silence, wondering if he'd made the right choice—or if he was just running from another fight he couldn't win.

The saloon was quieter than usual, the low murmur of conversation blending with the clink of glasses and the shuffle of boots on the worn wooden floor. Nash sat at a corner table, nursing a whiskey and watching the room with his usual detached air. His hat was tilted low, shadowing his eyes as he leaned back in his chair, one boot hooked over the rung of the opposite seat.

A man approached cautiously, a bottle of whiskey and a fresh glass in hand. The old miner was wiry, his back bent from decades of hard labor, his face weathered and lined like a map of his years in the pits. Despite the toll life had taken on him, there was a quiet determination in his step as he came up to Nash's table.

Wyatt Steele

"Evenin', cowboy," the miner said, his voice gravelly but steady.

Nash glanced up, his sharp gaze flickering over the man before he gave a small nod. "Evenin'."

The miner hesitated for a beat, then placed the fresh glass on the table and poured a generous measure of whiskey from the bottle. The amber liquid caught the light, glinting as it filled the glass. The miner set the bottle down and pushed the drink toward Nash.

"Reckon I owe you a drink," The miner said, his voice low enough not to carry to the rest of the room.

Nash raised an eyebrow but didn't immediately touch the glass. "Owe me?"

The man nodded, his hands resting on the back of the chair opposite Nash. "For what you did the other day. Stoppin' the Kane boys from settin' on Caleb like that." His voice softened. "Could've gone real bad for the kid if you hadn't stepped in."

Nash leaned forward slightly, picking up the glass and swirling the whiskey. "Didn't do it for thanks," he said evenly, though there was no edge to his tone.

"I figured as much," Jenkins replied, his lips twitching into a faint smile. "But you did it all the same. Not many folks in this town'd risk puttin' themselves between Kade's men and their next fight. My name is Jenkins, and I'm grateful we all are."

Revenge of the Gunfighter

Nash sipped the whiskey, savoring the smooth burn before setting the glass back down. "Kane boys got what was comin' to 'em," he said simply, his eyes steady on Jenkins. "What Caleb does next is up to him."

Jenkins chuckled softly, a dry, rasping sound. "Kid's got more guts than sense sometimes, but he's a good one. You gave him a chance to see another day. That's somethin'."

For a moment, the two men sat in silence, the hum of the saloon washing over them. Then Jenkins straightened, nodding toward the whiskey. "Figure you'll be needin' another before this place drives you half-mad."

Nash tipped his hat slightly, and the ghost of a smile tugged the corner of his mouth. "Much obliged."

As Jenkins shuffled away, Nash watched him for a moment, then leaned back in his chair, the glass still cradled in his hand. For all the town's broken spirit, there were still flickers of something worth protecting—however faint they might be.

Nash's room was dark, the only light spilling in from the thin sliver of moonlight that seeped through the warped wooden shutters. The night outside was still, save for the occasional creak of the saloon settling into its bones. Nash lay on the lumpy mattress, one arm draped over his eyes, his mind restless despite the quiet. Then he heard it.

A faint creak on the landing outside his door.

His body reacted before his mind caught up. In an instant, the Colt was in his hand, the cold metal familiar and steady. He slipped silently out of bed, the worn floorboards cool beneath his bare feet, and pressed himself against the wall behind the door. His breathing slowed, each inhale and exhale deliberate, controlled. His eyes, sharp and unrelenting, fixed on the door handle as it turned—slowly, deliberately.

The door creaked open a crack, the dim light from the hallway spilling in. Nash didn't wait to see who it was. With a sharp motion, he slammed the door hard into the figure trying to enter. There was a startled yelp, the sound of someone stumbling backward and hitting the floor. Nash stepped out from behind the door in a flash, his Colt aimed squarely at the intruder's chest.

"Don't move," he growled, his voice low and cold.

The figure on the floor groaned, one hand clutching the side of their head where the door had struck. "Damn it, Nash! It's me!" a familiar voice hissed, strained with pain.

Nash's eyes adjusted fully to the dim light, and his face fell as he realized who it was. "Sadie?" he muttered, lowering the Colt. He holstered it quickly and crouched down, offering her a hand.

Mumbling an apology, he helped her to her feet. She swayed slightly, one hand pressed to the side of her head where the edge of the door had cut into her skin. Blood trickled from the shallow wound, trailing down her temple, and her wide eyes shimmered with unshed tears. She wasn't crying from the pain, though—she looked more shocked than anything else.

"Hell, Sadie," Nash muttered, his voice rough with regret. "You shouldn't be sneakin' up on a man like that."

"I wasn't sneaking," she snapped, her voice wavering. "I didn't think you'd slam a door into me like a damn grizzly in a trap."

It was then Nash took in her appearance fully. She was wearing a thin, revealing bedrobe, the fabric clinging to her in a way that left little to the imagination. Her hair, usually tied back and neat, was loose, framing her face in messy waves. Nash frowned, his brow furrowing as he put two and two together.

"You were… you were hopin' to seduce me," he said bluntly, the realization landing hard. His tone was somewhere between bewildered and amused.

Sadie's cheeks flushed with heat, and she looked away, her jaw tightening. "Desperate times," she muttered, her voice barely above a whisper. "I'd do anything to be rid of Kade. Anything."

Nash leaned back slightly, one hand raking through his hair. "Well, damn," he said, his lips quirking into a lopsided grin. "Now I'm offended. Didn't realize women had to be desperate to sleep with me. Didn't think I was *that* bad."

Despite herself, Sadie let out a watery laugh, her composure cracking under the weight of the moment. But as quickly as it came, the laugh gave way to tears. Her shoulders shook, her breath hitching as the fear, frustration, and sheer exhaustion she'd been holding onto spilt over.

"I'm all out of courage, Nash," she choked, her voice breaking. "I don't know what else to do."

For a moment, Nash just stood there, watching her with a mixture of regret and understanding. Then, with a sigh, he stepped forward and wrapped his arms around her. She stiffened at first, but then she sank into the embrace, her head resting against his chest as her tears soaked into his shirt.

"It's alright," he said quietly, his voice softer now.

They stood like that for a long moment, the stillness of the room broken only by the faint sound of her sobs and the quiet murmurs of his reassurances. For all the fire and steel Sadie McAllister carried in her day-to-day, here she was, vulnerable and exposed, leaning on a man she barely knew because there was no one else left to turn to.

Nash tightened his hold on her, his own mind racing. He didn't know what the next step was, but he knew one thing for certain: this woman had been carrying the weight of the world on her shoulders for far too long. And maybe, just maybe, he could help her shoulder it—if only for a little while.

Sadie slept soundly that night, her breathing soft and steady as she lay curled against Nash. Her head rested on his shoulder, her auburn hair spilling across his chest like a warm cascade. One arm draped loosely over him, her fingers splayed against his ribcage as if she were anchoring herself to his presence.

Nash woke before the first light of dawn, the faint gray hues of the early morning creeping through the shutters. He stayed still, his eyes half-closed, savoring the rare moment of peace. It had been a long time since he'd woken to the warmth of another person beside him, and her arm resting across his chest stirred something he thought he'd buried long ago.

His hand moved instinctively, covering hers. Her skin was soft, her fingers relaxed against the calluses of his palm. He felt her breath against his neck—warm and even, stirring the faintest wisp of hair along his jaw. For a fleeting moment, he let himself lean into it, his eyes closing as he allowed the sensation to settle over him.

It felt good. Familiar. Almost like Emily.

His breath hitched, the memory cutting through the quiet. Emily, her laughter, her stubborn smile, the way she'd fit perfectly beside him like she belonged there. The ache of her absence was something he carried with him everywhere, but now, with Sadie so close, its weight pressed heavier than ever. His chest tightened, and the line between memory and reality blurred.

The urge to turn to Sadie was almost overwhelming. To brush her hair back from her face, to press his lips to hers, to lose himself for just a moment in the warmth she offered. His hand lingered on hers, his thumb brushing against her knuckles as his mind warred with itself.

But it wasn't Emily.

Swallowing hard, Nash forced himself to move. He gently lifted her arm, careful not to wake her, and slid out of bed. The cold morning air hit him as he stood, a stark reminder of where he was and who he was. Sadie murmured softly in her sleep, shifting slightly as her hand fell to the empty space where he'd been.

Nash rubbed a hand over his face, his jaw tight as he tried to shake off the moment. He crossed the room in a few quiet steps, retrieving his shirt and pulling it over his shoulders. The warmth of the bed, of Sadie, still clung to him, and for a second, he hesitated.

But there was no going back. Not to that bed.

He stepped to the window, leaning his forearm against the frame as he looked out at the pale horizon. His breath fogged the glass as he exhaled, steadying himself. Behind him, Sadie stirred slightly, still lost in sleep, and Nash closed his eyes for a brief moment.

He knew he'd made the right choice. But that didn't make it any easier.

CHAPTER FIVE

The morning sunlight spilled through the saloon's windows, casting long, golden streaks across the floor. Nash sat at a corner table, his mind preoccupied with the events of the night before.

Sadie emerged from the back room, her steps hesitant, her usual confident stride softened. Her auburn hair was tied back loosely, and a faint mark on her temple—the result of last night's mishap—stood out against her fair skin.

She cleared her throat, and Nash glanced up, immediately feeling the tension in the air.

"Morning," she said, her tone a little too casual as she moved to put coffee and a plate of breakfast on the table before him.

"Morning," Nash replied, his voice gruffer than usual. He straightened in his chair but avoided looking directly at her.

There was a beat of silence, broken only by the faint clink of glass against wood. Finally, Sadie turned, leaning on the table with forced nonchalance.

"You look like you didn't sleep much," she said, her eyes flickering toward him briefly before darting away.

"Yeah," Nash muttered, taking a slow sip of his coffee.

Revenge of the Gunfighter

Sadie hesitated, then gestured vaguely toward her temple. "Guess I've got you to thank for this."

Nash winced and set his cup down with a heavy clink. "Didn't mean for that to happen."

"I know," she said quickly, her lips twitching as if she was fighting a smile. "Just... not how I thought last night would go."

"Not how I thought it'd go either," Nash admitted, his voice low. His fingers tapped restlessly against the side of his mug. "Reckon I owe you an apology."

Sadie tilted her head, studying him. "Wasn't entirely your fault," she said after a moment. "I came in uninvited... and with, well, some ideas."

Nash rubbed the back of his neck, his face coloring slightly. "Yeah, I figured that much."

Sadie smirked despite herself, then winced as the motion pulled at her tender skin. She pressed a hand gently to the bruise, muttering, "You've got a hell of a way with woman, cowboy."

Nash huffed a dry laugh, shaking his head. "Figured you were one of Kade's men at first. Instinct kicked in."

"Must've been real disappointing to find out I wasn't," she said, arching an eyebrow.

He looked at her then, his expression softening. "Not disappointing," he said quietly. "Just... unexpected."

Another pause stretched between them, the awkwardness giving way to something unspoken. Sadie straightened and reached for a bottle, pouring herself a drink even though it was far too early for it.

"Well," she said, lifting the glass in mock salute, "here's to smoother encounters in the future."

Nash chuckled softly, tipping his coffee toward her in response. "Here's hopin'."

Sadie lingered for a moment longer, then turned back to her work. Nash leaned back in his chair, the tension in his chest loosening just a fraction. It wasn't much, but it was a start.

Later that day, Nash stood on the saloon porch, watching as a group of Kade's men strolled into the center of town. They moved with the easy confidence of predators, their rifles slung casually but ready for use. The miners emerged hesitantly from their homes and shops, clutching small bags of coins or goods to hand over.

One of Kade's enforcers, a broad-shouldered man with a cruel smile, grabbed a miner by the shirt, pulling him close. "This all you've got, old man?" he sneered, shaking the bag in his hand. "Kade doesn't take kindly to short pay."

The miner stammered, his face pale. "It's all I could spare. Please, my family—"

The enforcer slammed a fist into the man's gut, sending him crumpling to the ground. "Kade, don't care about your family. You find the rest, or we'll take it outta your hide."

Nash's jaw tightened, but he didn't move. His fingers brushed the handle of his Colt, but he knew better than to draw. Not yet.

A shout broke through the tense silence. "Leave him alone!"

Nash turned to see Caleb striding toward the scene, his fists clenched at his sides. His face was flushed with anger, his steps quick and determined.

"Caleb," Nash muttered under his breath, already moving to intercept him.
Before Caleb could reach the enforcers, Nash stepped in front of him, blocking his path. "Stop," he said, his voice low but firm.

"Get out of my way!" Caleb snapped, trying to push past him. "Someone's gotta stand up to them."

"Not like this," Nash said, gripping the younger man's arm. "You're not helping anyone by gettin' yourself killed."

"They can't just keep doing this!" Caleb shouted, his voice rising. "We have to fight back!"

Nash stepped closer, lowering his voice so only Caleb could hear. "You fight them now, it won't just be you they kill. They'll burn your house, hurt your family. Kade doesn't make examples—he wipes people out."

Caleb stared at him, his chest heaving with frustration. The fire in his eyes dimmed slightly as the weight of Nash's words sank in.

"Go home," Nash said. "Keep your head down."

Reluctantly, Caleb nodded and turned away, his shoulders slumping as he walked back toward the edge of town.

As Kade's men mounted their horses and rode off, their saddlebags full of stolen goods, Nash leaned against a post, his expression grim. He could feel the eyes of the townsfolk on him, their silent pleas hanging heavy in the air.

Sadie stepped out of the saloon, her face tight with anger. "You could've done something."

"And then what?" Nash asked, his tone cold. "I kill a couple of them, and Kade sends ten more. You think that solves anything?"

"So we're just supposed to take it?" Sadie snapped.

"For now," Nash said, though the words tasted bitter. "You don't pick a fight you can't win."

Sadie stepped closer, her expression sharp and accusing, cutting through Nash like a blade. But as he looked at her, his thoughts betrayed him. It wasn't Kade or the fight ahead that filled his mind—it was the memory of her warmth beside him, her breath soft against his neck in the stillness of the night. For a moment, he wanted to reach out, to brush his fingers against hers, to feel the quiet reassurance of her touch again. But the look on her face froze him in place. Sadie's eyes burned with disappointment, her jaw tight, and he knew exactly why.

"Maybe you're not the man I thought you were," she said, her voice low but cutting.

Nash swallowed hard, guilt twisting in his chest. He'd made his choice not to act, and now that choice sat heavy between them like an unspoken accusation.

Sadie shook her head, her shoulders stiff with frustration, and turned on her heel. As she walked away, Nash exhaled slowly, his hand twitching at his side as if it might reach for her even now.

His gaze shifted to the road where Kade's men had disappeared into the distance, the dust from their horses still hanging in the air. He reminded himself, as he always did, that he wasn't here to be a hero. He wasn't here to fight someone else's war.

Damn the woman, Nash thought, shaking his head as he leaned against the door frame. She might've stepped into his room last night with some fool plan to seduce him, and sure, it might've gone sideways—or so she probably figured. But damn her, she'd managed it all the same.

The memory of her, wrapped in that thin robe, her fiery hair loose and falling over her shoulders, wouldn't leave him alone. Her desperation, her vulnerability, the way she'd broken down in his arms—it stuck with him like a burr under the saddle. It wasn't just the softness of her touch or the warmth of her against him as she'd cried, though God help him, that part wasn't easy to forget. It was the way she'd looked at him, like he was the last solid thing in a world that was crumbling around her.

She'd gotten under his skin, and Nash hated it.

With a grunt of frustration, he pushed off the door frame, staring out at the dusty main street. A few townsfolk moved about their business, their heads low, their shoulders hunched. Blackrock was a town of ghosts, shadows of people too beaten down by Kade to stand tall anymore.

Damn, Sadie and her sharp tongue. Damn her courage, too, for coming into his room when she should've known better. And damn himself most of all for letting her in, for feeling something stir in his chest he hadn't felt since Emily. He rubbed a hand over his face, trying to scrub the thoughts away, but they lingered, persistent and unwelcome.

She thought her plan had failed, probably. That the whole seduction thing had backfired when she'd ended up crying in his arms instead. Nash gave a bitter chuckle, his fingers tapping restlessly on the window frame. She had no idea, did she? She might've thought she'd stumbled out of there with nothing but a cut on her head and a bruised pride, but she'd left something behind. Her. In his head. And worse, in his damned heart.

Nash shook his head again, the ghost of a rueful smile playing at his lips. "Damn her," he muttered, his voice low. She'd managed it alright. Whether he liked it or not.

Wyatt Steele

The acrid scent of smoke reached Nash before the shouting did, sharp and unmistakable as it carried on the evening breeze. He was leaning against the railing outside Sadie's saloon, one boot resting on the lower rung, his hat tipped low to block the last glare of the setting sun. But the smell of burning wood pulled his attention sharply.

Then came the cry. "Fire! Jenkins's place is burning!"

Nash's head jerked up, his eyes following the plume of smoke twisting into the darkening sky. It was thin at first, almost delicate, but it grew quickly, darkening into a thick, angry column. It rose from the far end of town, silhouetted starkly against the fiery hues of the sunset.

"They've hit Jenkins's place," someone shouted again, panic and despair thick in their voice.

Nash felt a hard knot twist in his gut. Jenkins was one of the older miners, a wiry man with a perpetually hunched back from years of hard labor underground, the only man brave enough in this damned town to have bought Nash a drink. Sadie had told Nash that Jenkins could barely keep up with the grueling demands of Kade's tribute system, but he always managed to scrape something together—always. Jenkins was no threat, just another broken piece of Blackrock trying to survive.

Now, his shack was ablaze.

Revenge of the Gunfighter

Nash strode down the steps of the saloon, his boots hitting the dirt with deliberate force. A small crowd had already gathered at a safe distance from the fire, their faces etched with helplessness and fear. The flames roared hungrily, devouring the dry wooden structure. Sparks flew into the air, carried on the breeze like angry fireflies, and the heat was fierce even from where Nash stood.

Kade's men were there too. Three of them leaned casually against their horses, their laughter loud and grating against the backdrop of the crackling fire. One of them, a hulking brute with a scar running down his cheek, tossed a cigarette into the dirt and ground it out with his boot heel as if to punctuate the destruction.

Jenkins stood in the middle of the street, his shoulders slumped, his face pale and slack with despair. He didn't cry or scream—he just stared, hollow and defeated, as the fire consumed everything he owned. His life, his hard-fought survival, was reduced to ash before his eyes.

Nash's fists clenched tightly at his sides. He could feel the tension coiling in his chest, the raw need to act, to put a bullet in the smirking bastards who stood there watching Jenkins's world burn. But he didn't move. Not yet. Not now. Starting a fight in the middle of the street would only end one way—with more bodies in the dirt. Nash knew that better than anyone. And he wasn't ready for it.

Wyatt Steele

Not yet.

Instead, he stood rooted where he was, the heat of the fire and the mockery of Kade's men burning into his skin as he watched the scene unfold.

Finally, as the roof of the shack caved in with a loud crash, sending a wave of sparks into the air, Kade's men their horses. They laughed as they rode out, their cruel voices echoing in the stillness that followed. The townsfolk stayed silent, their faces turned down to the dirt as the sound of hooves faded into the distance.

Nash exhaled slowly, forcing himself to relax his hands, though his knuckles still ached from the tension. The fire was dying now, reduced to smoldering embers and blackened timbers. But the damage had been done.

He glanced at Jenkins, still standing there, motionless. No one approached him, no one offered comfort or a helping hand. Fear kept them all frozen in place, and Nash felt a bitter anger rise in his chest—not just at Kade's men, but at the town itself, so broken and beaten that it couldn't even muster defiance.

Damn this place. Damn Kade. And damn himself for standing by. But Nash knew one thing—he wouldn't forget the laughter of those men, nor the look in Jenkins's eyes. Blackrock's silence might keep the peace, but it wouldn't last. Not if Nash had anything to say about it.

Revenge of the Gunfighter

Later, as the last embers of the fire smoldered in the twilight, Sadie stormed into the saloon, her eyes blazing with anger. She found Nash in the corner, nursing a drink, his face as unreadable as ever.

"You just stood there," she said, her voice sharp and accusing. "You let them burn his house to the ground."

Nash didn't look up. "Wasn't my fight."

Sadie slammed her hands on the table, making the glass jump. "Damn you, Nash! These people are suffering, and all you can do is sit there and drink like none of it matters? Someone snitched on Jenkins, he bought you a drink, and that's why he's been punished."

He finally met her gaze, his eyes cold and unflinching. "You think I don't know what it feels like to lose everything? You think I don't understand what it costs to fight men like Kade? I've paid that price, Sadie. And let me tell you, it's a hell of a lot more than you're ready for."

Her hands clenched into fists at her sides. "So what, you're just gonna let them take everything? Let them kill whoever they want? What kind of man are you?"

Nash stood, towering over her, his voice low and cutting. "The kind of man who knows that hope doesn't mean a damn thing against thirty hired guns. You want to stand up to Kade? Fine.

But don't you dare pretend it'll end anyway but bad?"

For a moment, neither of them spoke, the air between them charged with anger and frustration. Finally, Sadie shook her head, her voice trembling. "You're a coward, Nash. You talk like you've got all the answers, but all you're doing is running—from Kade, from yourself, from whatever it is you're so afraid to face."

She turned and walked away, leaving Nash alone at the table, her words ringing in his ears.

Nash watched her go, his jaw tightening as he fought to keep his composure. Her words had cut deep, sharper than he cared to admit, and yet, as his eyes followed her retreating figure, he felt something else stir in him—an almost overwhelming desire to haul her back, to silence her disapproving mouth with his own.

The worse her temper got, the more he wanted her, and it infuriated him. She had this way of cutting right to the heart of things, stripping away his defenses and leaving him raw. It wasn't just her words—it was her fire, her refusal to back down, even when he was certain she should.

Sadie turned at the door, her sharp gaze cutting across the room once more before she walked out, leaving Nash alone at the table. He exhaled sharply, running a hand over his face as her parting words echoed in his mind.

A coward. Running.

"Damn woman," he muttered under his breath, his fingers curling into a fist on the table. He hated how right she might be. And he hated even more that her fiery defiance was drawing him in like a moth to a flame.

The saloon felt emptier without her, but Nash didn't move. Instead, he sat there, her voice still ringing in his ears, a mix of anger, frustration, and something far more dangerous coursing through him.

As the saloon emptied out for the night, Nash sat in the quiet, staring into his drink. Sadie's accusation gnawed at him, not because it wasn't true, but because it was. He *was* running. From the ghosts of the ranch, from the weight of Emily's death, from the hollow ache of knowing he'd failed to protect the life they'd tried to build.

But Blackrock wasn't his problem. He told himself that over and over, trying to drown out the flicker of doubt that whispered otherwise.

Outside, the miners passed by in twos and threes, their faces shadowed in the dim light. Among them, Nash caught sight of Caleb, his shoulders hunched he glanced back toward the saloon, his eyes meeting Nash's for the briefest of moments.

Nash looked away. He couldn't afford to care.

Not again.

Wyatt Steele

CHAPTER SIX

The livery was quiet, save for the occasional snort or the soft scrape of hooves against the dirt floor. The smell of hay and leather hung thick in the air, the kind of familiar scent that always seemed to settle Nash's mind, even when the rest of the world refused to let him be. He ducked his head under the low beam as he stepped inside, his boots stirring dust as he made his way toward the far stall where his mare was stabled.

She whinnied softly when she saw him, ears pricking forward, her dark eyes watching him with calm familiarity. Nash managed a faint smile as he approached, reaching a hand over the gate to stroke the soft curve of her muzzle.

"Hey, girl," he murmured, his voice low and gentle. "You holdin' up all right?"

The mare huffed, nudging his hand as if to say, *Where've you been?* Nash chuckled under his breath, pulling a carrot he'd swiped earlier from his coat pocket and holding it out to her. She took it eagerly, the crunch of her teeth breaking the stillness. Nash leaned against the gate, letting his free hand trail along her neck, feeling the steady warmth of her beneath his fingers.

He'd had her for years—longer than he'd ever stayed in one place. She'd been with him through dust storms, freezing nights, and miles of empty trail. He remembered Emily laughing as they rode side by side. *"You take better care of that horse than yourself, Nash,"* she'd teased, her voice still ringing clear as a bell in his memory.

The smile on his face faded. Emily had been gone nearly two years, and it still didn't seem real some days. He closed his eyes, resting his forehead against the gate for a long moment, letting the ache in his chest settle deep. Time had worn down the edges of the pain, but it hadn't dulled it. It was still there, sharp and relentless, when it decided to show itself.

He ran a hand through his hair and exhaled, the sound low and heavy in the quiet. What would she think of him now? The things he'd done. The things he hadn't. He couldn't shake the thought of her—of them, riding out over the hills with the wind whipping past, free and full of dreams that didn't amount to much anymore.

But it wasn't just sadness that pulled at him now. It was something uglier.
Guilt.

He straightened, his hand slowing against the mare's neck. He wasn't a fool. He knew what it was that gnawed at him whenever Sadie McCallister walked into a room. That sharp-tongued woman with her stubborn stare and the fire in her voice. He didn't want to admit it—hell, he couldn't admit it—but there was something there. A pull, quiet and persistent. And he hated himself for it.

Was it because he missed Emily? The warmth of her smile, the feel of her lying next to him at night when the world outside seemed too much to bear? Or was it just some raw, physical need, the kind a man didn't think about until it got too loud to ignore? Nash swallowed hard, the thought sitting heavy in his gut.

It wasn't fair—to Sadie or to Emily. Wanting Sadie, even for a fleeting second, felt like a betrayal. A slap in the face to a woman who had given him her whole heart and died trying to bring his child into the world. He hadn't been able to save them. Couldn't protect them. So, what right did he have to want another woman? To even *think* about another woman?

"Damn it," Nash muttered, pulling his hand back and stepping away from the gate as if putting space between himself and the mare might quiet the storm in his head. He turned away, rubbing the back of his neck as he stared at nothing in particular.

The mare whinnied softly again as if she understood, and maybe she did. Nash looked back at her, the guilt twisting tighter in his chest. He didn't deserve peace. He didn't deserve warmth. He was a man meant for the trail, for the wind and dust and nothing else.

"Rest up, girl," he murmured, his voice quieter now. "We'll be ridin' soon enough."

Wyatt Steele

He gave her one last look before turning toward the livery door. The evening light spilled across the dirt floor as he stepped outside, the shadows lengthening as the sun sank lower in the sky. Nash jammed his hat back onto his head and walked into the fading light, trying—and failing—not to think about Emily, or Sadie, or the way his life seemed to hang somewhere in between.

As Nash left the stables from the far end of the street came shouts—angry and desperate. Nash's body stiffened as his eyes locked onto the commotion. Two of Kade's enforcers stood near the blacksmith's shop, their whips snapping through the air with vicious cracks. Between them was a young miner, no older than eighteen, his shirt ripped and his back already streaked with red from the lashes. He stumbled forward, trying to shield himself, but the larger of the two men drove a boot into his side, sending him sprawling into the dirt.

"You think you can short Kade?" the larger man sneered, raising his whip again. "You pay what you owe, boy, or you pay in blood."

The boy's cries pierced the oppressive silence, and Nash felt his stomach twist. He gritted his teeth, his hand brushing the butt of his Colt. *Stay out of it,* he told himself.

This ain't your fight.

Revenge of the Gunfighter

The scene triggered something deep within him, dragging him back to a memory he'd spent years trying to bury. A barren stretch of land. A man begging for mercy. And Nash, younger and more reckless, stood by while his former partner Luke Cain did what Nash hadn't had the guts to stop. Sure Cain had killed the attackers for pleasure, but still he'd done it.

Cain's voice, mocking echoed in Nash's mind. *You watch. You let it happen. So it'll be your fault.*

Nash clenched his fists, his jaw tightening as the memory dissolved. He wasn't that man anymore. He'd vowed to never stand idle in the face of cruelty again.

The enforcer brought the whip down again, the miner crying out in agony. Without thinking, Nash stepped out into the street. His boots crunched against the dirt, each step deliberate, his Colt already drawn.

"That's enough," he said, his voice cold and sharp.

Kade's men turned, their expressions shifting from annoyance to smug confidence as they recognized Nash. The larger man sneered, his whip coiled loosely in his hand. "This ain't your business, stranger. Walk away."

Nash didn't stop. He closed the distance slowly, his revolver steady in his grip. "I said, that's enough."

The smaller enforcer laughed, reaching for his pistol. "You're gonna regret—"

The crack of Nash's Colt cut through the air. The smaller man jerked backwards, a neat hole punched through his chest. He fell into the dirt, dead before he hit the ground.

The larger man roared in fury, drawing his own weapon, but Nash was faster. He fired again, the bullet catching the enforcer square in the throat. The man stumbled, gurgling as blood bubbled from the wound. He collapsed, his body twitching once before going still.

The street was deathly quiet. The townsfolk who had gathered to watch the spectacle now stood frozen, their faces pale. The young miner lay in the dirt, staring up at Nash with wide, disbelieving eyes.

Nash exhaled slowly, his revolver still smoking in his hand. He holstered it, turning to the boy. "Get up," he said gruffly.

The miner scrambled to his feet, wincing as he clutched his bruised side. "Th-thank you," he stammered, his voice shaking.

Nash didn't reply. He glanced around the street, his sharp eyes scanning for any sign of reinforcements. The tension in the air was palpable, the kind that came before a storm.

Nash stood in the street, the acrid smell of gunpowder still hanging in the air, his revolver smoking faintly at his side. Both men lay sprawled in the dirt, their weapons useless beside their lifeless hands. The town had gone deathly quiet, the silence pressing in from all sides as shutters creaked and doors eased open just a crack. Somewhere, a dog barked once, then fell silent.

Then the saloon doors burst open, and Sadie McCallister came rushing out, her skirts swishing angrily around her boots. "Nash!" she shouted, her voice shrill with disbelief. "What the hell have you done?"

Nash turned to her slowly, his face dark with anger, eyes sharp as flint. "What you *wanted* me to do," he growled, his voice low and biting. "That enough action for you?"

Sadie stopped dead in her tracks, stunned by his fury, her mouth opening like she meant to argue but nothing came out. Before she could respond, the sound of hurried boots echoed up the street, and Sheriff Hayes appeared, panting and wide-eyed as he skidded to a stop. His hat was askew, and his hand hovered near the pistol at his belt, though he looked like he had no idea what to do with it.

Hayes, his voice cracking as he took in the bodies sprawled on the ground. "Dear God, what have you *done*?"

Nash's lip curled into something that wasn't quite a smile. It was too hard, too bitter. He took a step forward, advancing on the sheriff, and Hayes instinctively stepped back, stumbling slightly.

Wyatt Steele

"I did what *you* should've done," Nash said, his voice deadly quiet, the words dripping with disdain. "I stopped those bastards from beatin' a man to death in the street while you sat on your ass."

The sheriff blanched, his eyes darting to the dead men in the dirt, then to Sadie, who stood frozen, looking between the two men.

"You don't get it, do you?" Nash went on, his anger spilling over like water from a broken dam. "You let this happen, all of it. Every bruise, every fire, every man forced to kneel to Kade—you let it happen. Don't stand there and look at me like I'm the problem."

Hayes stammered, his mouth opening and closing uselessly, but Nash didn't wait for a reply. He holstered his revolver, turned on his heel, and stalked straight past Sadie toward the saloon, his boots hammering the dirt.

"Nash!" Sadie called after him, her voice sharp, desperate. "Nash, wait—"

He didn't look back. He didn't stop. He stormed through the saloon doors, his fury like a storm cloud rolling off him. The few patrons who had dared to remain scattered, pulling back into the shadows as he moved behind the bar.

Nash grabbed a bottle of whiskey from the shelf, his hand closing around its neck like he meant to strangle it. With a sharp pop, he pulled the cork free and tossed it aside, not bothering to watch it bounce across the floor. He slammed a

Revenge of the Gunfighter

handful of coins onto the bar, the metal scattering and spinning on the wood.

"That oughta cover it," he muttered darkly.

Without waiting for a response, he turned and headed for the stairs, the bottle dangling from his hand as he stomped up to his room. Behind him, Sadie stood frozen in the saloon doorway, her face a mixture of shock, anger, and something else—something softer that she didn't dare let show.

The sheriff lingered behind her, his face pale and his hat clutched in his hands. "He's gonna get himself killed," Hayes muttered under his breath. "And probably take the whole town with him."

Sadie didn't respond. Her gaze stayed fixed on the stairs where Nash had disappeared, her expression unreadable.

From the landing above, a door slammed shut. A beat of silence followed, and then the low creak of a floorboard as Nash moved inside his room.

"Damn women," he muttered to himself as he sank onto the edge of the bed, taking a long pull of whiskey. The burn was harsh and welcome, but it didn't dull the fire in his chest, the anger that roared in his ears.

Sadie's face swam in his mind—the look of shock, of accusation, when she'd seen what he'd done. *Damn her* for asking for a fight and then looking at him like he was the villain when he delivered. Damn all of it. He'd done what was right—what needed doing—and still, it wasn't enough.

And yet, as he leaned back against the wall and tipped the bottle again, he couldn't shake the sound of her voice calling his name, or the look in her eyes when he'd stormed past her.

"Damn women," Nash muttered again, softer this time. The whiskey burned all the way down, but it couldn't touch the ache underneath.

CHAPTER SEVEN

The dim room was lit only by the fading orange glow bleeding through the thin curtains, the last light of day giving way to dusk. He stood for a moment, his silhouette stark against the pale walls, the whiskey bottle dangling loosely from his hand.

His eyes swept the room, landing on the bed. He crossed the creaking floorboards, tossing the bottle onto the small side table with a thud. The tension that coiled in his chest wasn't just anger—it was something sharper, a quiet certainty that the trouble he'd stirred up wasn't going to wait long to find him.

Without a word, Nash shrugged off his coat, his movements deliberate, almost ritualistic. He unbuckled his gunbelt and dropped it onto the bed with a soft thump, then moved to his saddlebag tucked near the foot of the bed. From it, he pulled his arsenal—each weapon placed on the rumpled blanket with careful precision. First came the Henry rifle, its stock worn smooth from years of use but still gleaming under the dim light. He set it down gently, its weight solid and reassuring.

Next, the Colt revolver—his second one—its familiar heft sliding easily into his hand before he laid it beside the rifle. A battered Peacemaker followed, the metal dulled but reliable, then an old

Wyatt Steele

Perry one-shot pistol, small but deadly, and finally a Smith & Wesson.

When he was done, the bed looked like a gunsmith's counter, his weapons lined up like old companions waiting for a fight. Nash exhaled through his nose, the sound low and steady, then reached for the whiskey and took another deep pull, the liquor burning down to his gut before he set the bottle aside.

Pulling a chair closer to the bed, he sank into it, rolling his sleeves to the elbows. There was work to be done. Trouble was on its way, and trouble deserved a proper welcome.

He picked up the Henry first, running his fingers along the polished barrel before opening it and inspecting the chamber. The rifle was clean—it always was—but Nash worked the oiled cloth over the metal anyway, the motions steady, methodical. He thumbed the cartridges one by one, sliding them in until the rifle was fully loaded. The quiet *snick* of each round settling into place filled the room like a clock ticking down.

When the Henry was set aside, he moved to the Colts. One after the other, he broke them open, spun the chambers, and checked the rounds. Six bullets each—full cylinders. He rubbed a patch of oil into the trigger guard of the Peacemaker next, letting his thoughts drift as he worked. Emily's voice crept into his thoughts, soft but sharp, the kind of memory that stuck like a thorn, it was something she'd said to him just after they'd first met, and maybe it was true. *"You treat those guns like they're old friends, Nash. Maybe you'd still have some if you took care of people the same way."*

He swallowed hard, pushing the thought away.

He couldn't afford distractions.
Not tonight.

As he worked his way down the line, each weapon was cleaned, inspected, loaded, and placed carefully back on the bed, ready for what was coming. He knew the men he'd killed today weren't the kind Kade would let go unanswered. They'd be back—tonight, maybe tomorrow—but they'd come, guns in hand, vengeance in their eyes.

When the Smith & Wesson was ready, Nash sat back in the chair, his hands resting on his thighs. The whiskey sat at his elbow, but he didn't reach for it now. Instead, he stared down at the weapons spread before him, the light catching on their barrels like faint streaks of silver. Each one had a story to tell, just like the scars on his skin or the lines etched into his face.

He could feel it in his bones—that old, familiar hum of anticipation that came before a fight. There was no peace to be had here, not anymore. The moment he'd pulled the trigger in the street, Blackrock had become a battlefield, and Nash wasn't the type to walk away before it was done.

Wyatt Steele

The wooden floorboards creaked beneath Nash's boots as he thundered down the stairs, the weight of his arsenal making each step echo through the empty saloon. The Henry rifle was slung across his back, the barrel peeking up over his shoulder, while the twin Colts sat snug in their holsters at his hips. The Smith & Wesson was tucked into his belt, and the small Perry pistol rested against his chest, hidden beneath his vest. His second gun belt rode low, worn and heavy with extra rounds. In one hand, he carried the whiskey bottle, the glass catching the light from the low lamps as he moved.

When he hit the bottom of the stairs, the batwing doors creaked, and Sadie strode in like a woman on a mission. Her sharp gaze landed on Nash, narrowing slightly at his appearance—armed to the teeth, whiskey in hand, looking every bit the man ready for war. She didn't say anything at first, just dropped the weapons she carried onto a table with a loud clatter. Two pistols, taken from Kade's men, heavy and still marked with dust and blood. Over her shoulder were their gun belts, the leather creased and worn from years of use.

"Brought these," Sadie said, her tone brisk, though there was a tension under it she couldn't quite hide. "Figured they might come in handy."

Nash eyed the weapons, the corners of his mouth twitching faintly—not quite a smile, but close enough. "Not bad," he muttered, taking a swig from the bottle before setting it down with a thud on the nearest table.

Behind Sadie, Caleb appeared, breathless and nervous, his boots scuffing loudly on the floor as he stepped inside. He looked from Sadie to Nash, his face pale but determined. "What do you need me to do?" he asked, his voice wavering just slightly.

Nash turned, his gaze hard as flint. "I need every man in Blackrock who can hold a gun and stand on two legs in here, now. Bring every rifle, revolver, and box of ammunition this town has to offer. We don't have long."

Caleb swallowed hard, his hands clenching at his sides. "You think they'll come back that quick?"

Nash's jaw tightened. "They're not the kind to let two of their men lie cold in the dirt without payin' the rest of us a visit. Now get moving."

Caleb nodded, turning on his heel and rushing out of the saloon, his footsteps pounding on the wooden boards as the batwing doors flapped wildly behind him.

Nash turned back to Sadie, who was still watching him, her expression a mixture of apprehension and approval. Her eyes flicked to the weapons strapped across his body, the steel glinting in the low light. "You really think we stand a chance?" she asked quietly.

Nash grabbed one of the pistols she'd brought, spinning it once before breaking it open to check the rounds. "We don't have to win a war," he said grimly, snapping the gun closed and tucking it into the pile of weapons. "We just have to make sure Kade and his men think twice before they come back here again."

Nash glanced around the saloon with a critical eye, his gaze lingering on the thin wooden walls, the large windows, and the narrow staircase that led to the rooms upstairs. His jaw tightened. "This place isn't ideal to be holed up in."

Sadie, standing behind the bar, narrowed her eyes. "What's wrong with it?"

"Too many ways in." Nash stepped toward the back door, testing the handle before letting it fall back into place. "The back needs to be barred shut—something heavy, furniture or a beam if you've got one. If they get in from behind, we're done for." He turned and pointed toward the windows on either side of the saloon. "And it's too close to those two buildings out there. Kade's men could climb from their rooftops and onto the balconies upstairs. That's where they'll try to come at us."

Sadie crossed her arms, brow furrowing as she followed his gaze. "So what do we do about it?"

Nash motioned to the staircase leading to the second floor. "We seal off the stairs. Haul up a couple of tables and block 'em tight. If they want in bad enough, they'll have to make noise breaking through. That'll buy us time." His voice was steady, but grim. "We're not fighting to win, Sadie. We're fighting to make 'em change their minds—take a few of them down until they decide it's not worth the trouble. That's the best shot we've got."

"And if they don't change their minds?" she asked, her voice low, like she already knew the answer.

Nash's expression didn't shift. "Then it won't matter."

Sadie stared at him for a beat, then turned on her heel and disappeared behind the bar. She returned a moment later, shotgun in hand, two heavy boxes of cartridges balanced against her hip. Setting them down on one of the tables with a dull thud, she slid the shotgun open, checked it, and snapped it shut with a practiced hand.

"Then let's make 'em pay for every damn bullet," she said, her voice cold and sharp.

Nash nodded approvingly. He stepped forward and began dragging the saloon's tables into place, creating a makeshift barricade in front of the saloon doors. Once the tables were lined up, he placed the guns across the surface—Colts, a Smith & Wesson, and her worn shotgun—and set boxes of ammunition beside each. He picked up the belts Sadie had brought, coiling them and setting them alongside the line of guns. The layout was clean and deliberate, like tools waiting for a craftsman.

When he finished, Nash looked up at Sadie, his face serious, his tone flat but firm. "You keep them loaded, and I'll keep firing 'em."

"Don't you worry about that," she said. "I can handle my end."

For a moment, neither of them spoke, the weight of what was coming hanging heavy in the silence. Nash finally stepped back, rolling the sleeves of his shirt to his elbows as he surveyed the room.

It wasn't much of a fortress. But it would have to do.

"Damn women," he muttered to himself, though there was no heat in the words this time—only a resigned acceptance.

CHAPTER EIGHT

The saloon was quiet for a long beat, the air heavy with anticipation. Outside, the town was waking up to what was coming. Soon enough, the silence would be replaced by the clatter of boots and the low click of hammers being drawn back.
And Nash would be ready.

"Come on, then," he muttered under his breath, his voice low and dangerous. "Let's see what you've got."

Sadie grabbed her shotgun from the table, and she turned toward the saloon doors, her boots striking the wooden floor with purpose. Nash, still standing near the makeshift barricade of tables, frowned and straightened up.

"Where are you going?" he demanded, suspicion edging his tone.

Sadie glanced back over her shoulder, her expression set. "To fetch the sheriff."

Nash's brows rose in disbelief. "You think that coward's gonna join us?"

Sadie's lips curled into a small, knowing smile. "Whether you like it or not, Nash, he's gonna be here. Even if I have to drag him by his ear."

Nash stared at her for a beat, then let out a low, rumbling chuckle. "You're somethin' else, Sadie."

She just shrugged, cocking the shotgun with a click, then pushed through the batwing doors and disappeared. Nash watched her go, his grin lingering as he shook his head. *Damn woman,* he thought, though there was something like admiration glinting in his eyes.

The door had barely settled before Caleb stumbled back into the saloon, his face flushed, breathing hard. He skidded to a halt just inside, looking around as if unsure where to stand. Behind him came two men, rough and dirt-streaked miners with the weight of their years carved into their faces. One was lanky and sharp-featured, his dark hair shot through with gray—Caleb introduced him as Jake Black. The other was stockier, with wide shoulders and a sun-scarred face, Ket Marley.

Caleb looked at Nash apologetically, his hands fiddling at his sides. "I—I'm sorry, Nash. I could only get these two to come. Everyone else... they're hidin'."

Nash glanced at the men. Both carried their own guns—Jake's a long-barreled revolver that had seen better days, Ket's a shotgun with a cracked stock. They looked tired, grim, but resolute. Nash nodded in acknowledgement.

"Can't blame the rest of 'em," Nash said finally, his tone even. "But you two"—he pointed a finger at Jake and Ket—"I appreciate you bein' here. Takes guts to step up when no one else will."

Jake Black adjusted the grip on his revolver, his expression calm, almost casual. "Hell, mister, we're the ones thankin' *you*. You didn't have to take an interest in this mess."

Ket Marley grunted in agreement, resting the shotgun against his shoulder. "Blackrock's been dyin' slow for years, and we just sat back and let it happen. Took an outsider to remind us what standin' up looks like."

Nash's jaw tightened at that, his gaze dropping briefly to the floor. He didn't answer right away. Truth was, he *wouldn't* have taken an interest—not normally. If Kade's men had come for the town earlier, Nash would've ridden out, never looking back. But waking up to find Sadie beside him, warm against his shoulder, her arm draped across his chest—it had stirred something. A memory he hadn't wanted, a yearning he thought he'd buried. Whether it was pride, guilt, or just the ghost of Emily lingering in his heart, it didn't matter.

Nash finally exhaled, clearing his throat and shoving those thoughts aside. He looked back up at the two miners and offered a small, gruff nod. "Well, you're here now. That's what counts."

Ket tipped his head, and Jake gave a faint smile before wandering toward one of the tables to inspect the weapons Nash had laid out. Caleb lingered a moment, watching Nash carefully as if trying to understand what made the drifter tick.

"You okay, Nash?" he asked quietly.

Nash just glanced at him and snorted, pulling his hat lower over his eyes. "Long as there's whiskey and bullets, I'll manage."

He turned his back on the boy, pretending to busy himself with the Henry rifle, but his hands faltered for just a second. *Damn woman,* he thought again, feeling something uncomfortable settle in his chest. She was trouble, just like this town. And yet, here he was.

It wasn't the fight that kept him here. It was her.

The saloon doors swung open with a loud creak, cutting through the uneasy silence. Nash glanced up from the table where he was checking the load on his Henry rifle, his expression hardening as Sadie marched back into the room. Behind her, Sheriff Amos Hayes shuffled in reluctantly, his face twisted into a scowl, like a man dragged into something he wanted no part of. His tin star caught the dim light as he moved, but there was nothing of a lawman's pride in the way he carried himself—just resignation and bitterness.

"Here he is," Sadie said briskly, jerking her thumb toward Hayes. Her tone was sharp, her frustration barely hidden. "Told you I'd bring him."

Nash's gaze flicked from her to the sheriff, his brow furrowing. "You didn't say he'd come kickin' and screamin'."

"I'm here, ain't I?" Hayes barked, his face flushed with anger and embarrassment. He swiped off his hat and smacked it against his leg, sending a puff of dust into the air. "Damn woman threatened to put a shotgun to my back if I didn't come. I'm too damn old for this."

Sadie crossed her arms and shot him a glare. "You're too damn scared, you mean."

Hayes whirled on her, his mustache bristling. "Watch yourself, Sadie. I didn't take this badge just to get shot dead in the street for a lost cause."

"A lost cause?" Sadie's voice rose, fierce and sharp as flint. "That's all this town's been since you let Elijah Kade run roughshod over it. You sit in that office of yours with a bottle in one hand and excuses in the other while people like Jenkins lose their homes. *Good men*."

Hayes opened his mouth to argue, but Nash cut in, his voice low and cold. "So you're just gonna stand back and let Kade burn the rest of this place down? Watch him whip kids and tear apart families?" He took a step closer, his eyes narrowing. "Hell of a sheriff you turned out to be."

Hayes stiffened, the insult landing hard. For a moment, Nash thought the man might storm right back out the door. Instead, Hayes looked down at the scuffed floorboards, his face dark with shame. "It's not that simple, and you know it," he muttered. "A man can't stand up to thirty guns alone."

"No," Nash said flatly, "but a man with a spine might've done something before it came to this."

Hayes' eyes shot up, glowering at Nash. "You think you're some kind of savior, don't you? Some gun-totin' hero here to fix the mess the rest of us can't."

Nash didn't blink, didn't flinch. "I don't think I'm anything," he replied coolly. "But I know one thing for certain—I'm not a coward."

Hayes' fists balled at his sides, but Sadie stepped between them before things could boil over. "Enough," she snapped, her tone brooking no argument. "We don't have time for this. Kade's men'll be here before we know it, and this town needs every warm body with a gun. So you're here, Amos—like it or not."

The sheriff grunted, turning away as he shoved his hat back on his head. "This ain't gonna end well," he muttered. "But fine. I'm here."

Nash shook his head, disgusted but not surprised. He turned to Sadie. "You're determined to drag the whole damn town into this, aren't you?"

Sadie leveled him with a glare, her chin tilted defiantly. "Somebody has to."

Revenge of the Gunfighter

Nash studied her for a moment, the fire in her eyes burning brighter than the lamplight in the saloon. He couldn't decide if she was brave or just plain foolish. Maybe both.

"Caleb and two others are upstairs looking out for trouble, when they see it they'll come down and we'll block off the stairs," Nash said finally, his voice gruff. "We're makin' a stand whether it ends well or not."

Sadie gave a small nod before turning her attention back to the sheriff, who was still hovering near the door, his hand resting nervously on the revolver at his hip. "You stick close, Amos. If you're gonna wear that star, you might as well *use* it."

The sheriff muttered something under his breath, but Nash was already moving, his boots thudding heavily as he picked up the Henry and slung it back over his shoulder. He paused at the table, checking the scattered guns and ammunition one more time. Trouble was coming, and there was no time left for hesitation.

As Sadie crossed the room, Nash glanced at her briefly, his voice low. "You really think the sheriff's gonna be any help?"

She shrugged, though her jaw was set with determination. "I think he'll be what he needs to be when the bullets start flying."

Nash almost smiled at that, though there was no humor in it. He turned and headed for the staircase to check on Caleb and the others, muttering under his breath as he went.

"Damn women…"

Nash glanced back at Sadie. She was moving with purpose across the saloon, checking the weapons and ammunition he'd laid out, barking an order at the sheriff when he hesitated near the door. She was all fire and sharp edges—determined, stubborn, and relentless.

But even now, as she shoved a box of shells toward the sheriff, there was something about her that Nash couldn't ignore. Her hair, loose from its usual tie, tumbled over her shoulders in wild auburn waves, catching the light in a way that made it look almost molten. She wore a man's shirt, the sleeves rolled up and the hem tucked hastily into her skirts, but the curves of her body were still plain as day, impossible to hide. Nash swallowed hard, a flicker of a memory flashing through his mind—Sadie in her thin nightgown, standing in his room, her head bleeding, her body trembling, and him trying to forget the softness he'd seen beneath the fabric.

He looked away quickly, cursing himself under his breath. *Damn it, Nash.*
She didn't know, he told himself—didn't know she was driving him crazy. Didn't know that every time she stormed into a room, her eyes blazing and her chin tipped in defiance, she sparked something inside him he'd thought was long dead. Every time

she stood close, her scent—lavender—made his pulse kick up a little faster than he liked to admit.

And if she *did* know? Nash figured it'd be just another way she could twist the knife. He shook his head. This wasn't the time for foolish thoughts. Trouble was coming fast, and he needed a clear head.

Still, he glanced back one last time. Sadie had paused at the bar, the light catching the determined line of her jaw. Nash exhaled slowly, forcing himself to look away, frustrated—at her, at himself, at whatever this thing was that had begun to gnaw at the edges of his resolve.

CHAPTER NINE

The air inside the saloon thickened, the weight of impending violence settling like dust. Caleb's boots thundered down the stairs, followed closely by Jake Black and Ket Marley, their faces pale but determined.

"They're coming!" Caleb gasped, his voice hoarse with tension. "Coming straight down the street, we counted eight of them."

Nash didn't waste time, and gestured toward the staircase. "Get it barricaded. Now."

Caleb and the others sprang into motion, dragging tables, chairs, and whatever else they could find into a ramshackle blockade. Nash joined them, shoving a heavy barrel into place. The wood groaned as it scraped across the floorboards.

"This is it," Nash said, his voice calm despite the tension that coiled in his gut. "Make it count."

The saloon fell into silence, save for the sound of labored breathing and the quiet click of Jake Black checking his rifle. Nash moved to one of the windows, his steps deliberate, and pulled back the edge of the curtain just enough to see.

Kade's men were easy to spot, riding up the street like they owned it. Eight of them, their horses' hooves stirring up the dry dust of

Blackrock's main street. They fanned out in front of the sheriff's office, shouting for Hayes, but it didn't take them long to realize the place was empty.

Nash leaned back, letting the curtain fall into place. Caleb looked up from where he crouched behind the barricade, sweat dripping from his brow. "What are they doing?"

"They're coming here." Nash picked up his Henry rifle, already loaded and ready, and moved toward the batwing doors. "Eight of 'em."

Caleb let out a shuddering breath. "Eight...?"

"Eight's a good number," Nash said, lowering his voice as if it might steady the kid's nerves. He crouched by the doors, angling the rifle on the wood, his movements slow and methodical. "Keep your eyes sharp, though. More might be coming. But eight? I can handle eight."

Caleb swallowed hard, staring at him. "You can handle *eight*?"

Nash's mouth tugged into something that might've been a smile if the stakes weren't so high. "I won't need to. You drop four of Kade's men, the rest will scatter like rats. Nobody here's dying for Elijah Kade."

Jake Black murmured his agreement, gripping his old revolver. "He's right. Take a few of 'em, and the others'll run."

Wyatt Steele

Nash stared back out at the street. He could hear the horses now, their hooves slowing, pacing uneasily as the riders approached the saloon. Then, as if from nowhere, a voice rattled through his mind, cold and familiar.

Luke Cain.

"Don't wait for the first shot, Nash," Cain's voice whispered like a devil on his shoulder. "Survivors don't play fair. Get the first hit in, every damn time."

Nash tightened his grip on the Henry, his heart thudding slow and heavy in his chest. Cain had been right—still was. This wasn't the time to wait, wasn't the time for caution. The men outside weren't the type to hesitate, and giving them the chance to fire first would be suicide.

Nash set the barrel of the Henry on the edge of the batwing door, steadying it with both hands. Through the narrow slit of space, he lined up his first shot. One of Kade's men—broad-shouldered, wearing a filthy duster—sat tall in the saddle, scanning the building with a sneer.

Nash exhaled slowly.

Survivors don't play fair.

The Henry barked, the crack of the shot splitting the air.

The man's body jolted backwards as the bullet punched into his chest. He tumbled off his horse, landing in the dust with a lifeless thud. The animal bolted, spooked by the gunfire, and chaos erupted.

Before they could react, Nash fired again, this shot less clean—it clipped another rider's arm, and the man cried out, his body pitching sideways as blood streaked down his sleeve. The others pulled hard on their reins, yelling to each other in panic.

"Get back!" one of them shouted.

Their hesitation didn't last long. The front of the saloon exploded with return fire, bullets punching through the wooden walls and splintering the batwing doors. Nash ducked back instinctively, the Henry still clutched in his hands, as a hail of lead tore into the room.

"Down!" he barked. Caleb, Jake, and Ket scrambled for cover, their faces pale as the gunfire rattled the walls like a drum.

Nash crouched behind an overturned table, his breathing steady as splinters and dust rained down around him. He checked the Henry, his lips pressing into a thin line. Two shots gone. Still plenty left.

"They ain't happy!" Jake shouted from across the room.

Nash smirked faintly. "Good."

The barrage stopped as quickly as it had started, leaving a ringing silence in its wake. Nash risked a glance out the shattered doors and saw Kade's men regrouping in the street, hunkering down behind a wagon.

"Caleb," Nash said sharply, his voice cutting through the quiet. "Keep watch for more. I don't want any surprises."

Caleb nodded, sliding to the window, his rifle at the ready.

Nash's eyes narrowed as he watched the street. Eight men. One down, another bleeding. *It was a start.* But they'd be back, and they'd come harder next time. Nash couldn't shake the feeling that this was just the beginning.

They'll be back.

Nash knew that as sure as he knew his own name. Kade's men would regroup, and when they came, it wouldn't be with idle threats or slow approaches. They'd hit hard, looking for any crack they could find to push their way in.

The silence outside was suffocating. For now, the gunfire had stopped, the smoke from the street drifting in soft, ghostly plumes through the gaps in the doors. Inside the saloon, the air was thick with sweat, whiskey, and a powdery haze that stung the eyes.

Caleb was crouched behind a stack of barrels, positioned so he could see down the street, his rifle trembling slightly in his hands. Jake and Ket were stationed farther down, both miners pale but determined, gripping their weapons as though their lives depended on them—which they did. Sadie stood with the sherrif behind the bar with her shotgun, two boxes of cartridges within reach, her eyes fixed on Nash for what to do next.

"Quiet," Nash said suddenly, his voice low.

They all froze, listening.

Then they heard it—faint at first, the sound of movement. Around the back of the saloon.

Sadie's head whipped toward Nash, her brow furrowed with worry.

"They're testing it," Nash muttered. "Looking for a way in."

The back door was barricaded tight, the tables they'd piled against it groaning under the weight of the lock and crossbar. The saloon had been built sturdy, but Nash knew better than to trust wood against men that desperate.

The noise at the back faded, replaced by a new sound. Above.

Boots.

The boards of the balcony creaked faintly, then again. Kade's men were up there now, trying their luck with the second floor.

Sadie's eyes shot toward the staircase barricade they'd thrown together earlier. Heavy tables, barrels, and chairs had been wedged into place. It would take a man a few minutes of noisy fumbling to get through that tangle—and anyone stupid enough to try would make an easy target.

The boots upstairs paused, then scuffled again.

Nash stepped back from the batwing doors, his Colt already in his hand. His eyes drifted toward the ceiling, narrowing as he listened carefully. He closed his eyes for a moment, tuning out the nervous breathing of the others and the faint whistle of wind through the bullet-pocked window.

Boot. Step.

Another.

Nash tracked the sound of movement across the floor above, mapping the steps out in his mind. Someone was creeping carefully across the boards, slow and deliberate—trying not to give away their position.

Another step.

Nash's eyes snapped open.

Without a word, he aimed the Colt upward and fired.

The first shot shattered the silence, a deafening crack that made the whole saloon jump. Sadie ducked instinctively as plaster exploded from the ceiling, dust raining down like fine snow.

The boots stumbled above. Nash fired again. And again.

Three more shots barked from the Colt, each one well-aimed, blasting holes through the floorboards above.

There was a sharp, pained yell from upstairs, followed by a dull thud as a body hit the floor.

Sadie let out a startled yelp as a cloud of plaster dust and wood chips rained down across the bar.

"Damn it, Nash!" she hissed, throwing up an arm to shield her face. "You're gonna bring the whole damn roof down!"

Nash ignored her, his ears straining for more movement.

Silence.

The footsteps had stopped. Whoever was still up there was smart enough to realize they'd be next if they so much as sneezed.

Nash exhaled slowly, the acrid scent of gunpowder thick in the air.

From behind the barricade, Caleb's voice trembled. "Did—did you get him?"

"Don't know," Nash replied gruffly, reloading his Colt with calm, practiced hands. "But I sure as hell gave him something to think about."

Jake Black, crouched by the window, gave a low whistle, his face pale beneath the layer of grime. "Ain't seen shootin' like that in my life."

Sadie scowled, brushing debris out of her hair. "You're gonna bring the whole saloon down on our heads."

Nash allowed himself the faintest hint of a smile, the adrenaline cooling in his veins. "You're welcome, Sadie."

She glared at him, but he caught the flicker of relief behind her frustration.

From outside, the street remained eerily still. Kade's men weren't fools; they'd heard those shots and knew that whatever awaited them inside the saloon wasn't worth charging headlong into. At least, not yet.

Nash took a step back, rolling his shoulder to ease the tension. He tossed a glance toward Caleb and the others, their faces still taut with fear and uncertainty.

"This ain't over," he said quietly. "They're regroupin'. But we've bought ourselves a little time."

Sadie frowned, still shaking dust from her hair. "Time for what?"

Nash holstered his Colt and glanced back at the ceiling, his expression grim. "To make 'em regret comin' back."

Two down, and one bleeding.

The saloon remained eerily still, the only sound the creak of wood and the soft, nervous breaths of Caleb and the others. Then the faint *clink* of metal outside pulled his focus back to the street.

From the corner of the batwing doors, he risked a glance. What he saw made his jaw tighten.

Kade's men had hitched up a team to one of the mine wagons from the edge of town—thick, heavy, and built to haul loads of solid rock. It groaned forward, the wheels grinding against the dry dirt as they hauled it straight up the center of the street.

"Damn it," Nash muttered under his breath.

The wagon rolled closer, moving deliberately. Kade's men were using it as a rolling shield, pressing their advantage. Nash could see the shapes of riders flanking it on either side, rifles in their hands, but the solid wood wagon blocked any clean shot.

Sadie, crouched behind the bar, craned her neck to peek through a cracked window. "What are they doing?" she asked, her voice edged with tension.

"They're bringin' cover," Nash replied tersely.

Through the haze of settling dust and lingering smoke, he watched as the wagon lurched to a stop about twenty yards from the saloon.

"Not good," Caleb murmured, his face paling as he crouched with his rifle near the barricaded staircase.

"They're too damned close," Nash growled.

Outside, Kade's men moved quickly, already untethering the horses from the wagon.

Nash knew why—they didn't want the animals spooking under gunfire and dragging the cover away. Smart. Too smart.

The sharp whistle of one of Kade's men cut through the stillness.

"Go! Now!"

The shout was followed by a barrage of gunfire. Rifles cracked and bullets punched through the front of the saloon, splintering wood and shattering glass.

"Down!" Nash barked, pressing his back against the batwing doors as splinters rained over him.

Five men broke from cover behind the wagon, moving low and fast, their boots kicking up clouds of dust. They ducked in behind the mine wagon, huddling close to its thick wooden sides. Nash could see the heavy, reinforced planks—they'd take far more than a bullet to punch through.

"Damn it," he hissed.

Sadie's shotgun roared as she fired blindly over the bar, the echo deafening in the small space. "They're right on top of us!"

"We can see that, Sadie!" Nash snapped back, sweat dripping down the back of his neck.

The saloon's front wall creaked under the relentless fire, bullets chewing through posts and planks. Kade's men were pressing their advantage hard now, keeping the defenders pinned.

"Caleb!" Nash shouted over the din. "Keep your eyes open—if more of 'em show up, we're finished!"

Caleb flinched as a bullet smacked into the staircase barricade, sending shards of wood flying past his face. "They're close enough already!"

Nash ignored him. He darted low along the floorboards, slipping behind the bar where Sadie crouched, reloading with steady hands.

"What do we do now?" she demanded, her knuckles white around the shotgun stock.

Nash's mind raced as he pulled his Colt and checked the rounds. "We hold," he said simply. "And we make every bullet count."

From behind the cover of the bar, Nash peered through a narrow break in the wood, his sharp gaze locking on the wagon. Kade's men crouched behind it, confident in their cover, firing in bursts at the saloon windows and doors. Every now and then, one of them leaned out to take a shot, but the wagon itself blocked nearly every angle of attack.

Nash gritted his teeth. He had to thin them out before they got any bolder.

Closing one eye, he leveled his Colt carefully through the gap. One of the men popped out from behind the wagon to fire—Nash squeezed the trigger. The Colt barked, and the man jerked sideways, a crimson spray marking where the bullet found its mark.

The man fell, dead weight collapsing into the dirt.

"You got one!" Caleb shouted from his position, his voice full of hope.

From behind the wagon, another of Kade's men bellowed angrily. "Keep firing! Pin 'em down!"

The gunfire resumed with renewed ferocity. Bullets thudded into the saloon, shattering more glass and splitting beams. Nash ducked lower, his ears ringing as plaster crumbled from the ceiling.

"Think you can set the wagon on fire?" Sadie yelled, her voice hoarse.

Nash gave her a sharp look. "Not unless you're hiding dynamite under the bar, Sadie."

The front of the saloon was getting torn apart, the walls sagging under the punishment. Nash could feel the pressure closing in, and with every shot that punched through the wood, he knew their time was running out.

"We can't stay here forever," Caleb called out, his voice frantic.

Nash crouched lower, peeking through the window again. Kade's men were still holed up behind the wagon, emboldened now, thinking they had the upper hand.

Maybe they did. But Nash wasn't about to let them have it easy.

"Sadie," he said, pulling back the hammer on his Colt, "I'm gonna make 'em think twice."

Sadie looked at him like he'd lost his mind, but she nodded, gripping the shotgun tightly.

Nash took a deep breath, calming himself. Then, in a burst of motion, he rose from behind the bar, firing his Colt as fast as he could pull the trigger.

The sharp cracks of gunfire split the air as Nash sent bullets toward the wagon, forcing Kade's men to duck and scramble for cover. Sadie was right behind him, her shotgun roaring like thunder as she pumped rounds over the bar.

For a moment, the air was chaos—screams, gunshots, and the splintering of wood.

One of Kade's men shouted in pain, a bullet finding its mark. Another cursed loudly, yelling for the others to hold their fire and regroup.

Nash dropped back behind the bar, his Colts empty. He tossed it to Sadie, who fumbled to reload it as quickly as her hands would allow.

"You're insane," she panted, sweat streaking her face.

Nash managed a grim smile. "That's been said."

Nash checked his weapons—two Colts, the Smith & Wesson snug against his belt—

and he slipped his knife from its sheath. The gunfire outside had stilled, but silence didn't mean safety. Moving carefully, he approached the makeshift barricade at the bottom of the staircase. His boots made barely a sound as he crept around the edge of the barricade, his sharp gaze locked on the dim, shadowy steps above.

He was certain there was still one of Kade's men upstairs. Maybe wounded, maybe not. Either way, he couldn't leave him there.

Nash moved slowly, each step deliberate as he placed his weight carefully to avoid the old wood creaking beneath him. The stairwell smelled faintly of dust and smoke, every shadow seeming deeper in the low light. Sweat slicked the back of Nash's neck as he climbed, his knife tight in his hand.

At the top of the stairs, he paused, listening. A faint movement to his left—a shuffling sound, a boot scraping against the floor. Nash's eyes narrowed, and he flattened against the wall.

He's watching the fight, Nash thought.

He crept closer, careful to keep his breathing even. There, in a corner room with a shattered window, one of Kade's men crouched, rifle in hand. And another lay dead face down on the floor. The man leaned forward, resting the barrel on the sill as he scanned the street below. Nash could see his tensed shoulders and the way he shifted for a better view.

Moving with the fluid precision of a predator, Nash slid across the floor, his boots quiet on the boards. He crept up behind the man, knife raised, every nerve in his body focused on what came next.

The moment the man shifted his weight slightly to the side, Nash struck.

His arm shot around the man's throat, yanking him back with one sharp tug. Before the man could scream, Nash pressed the cold steel of his blade against his neck and pulled. The man's body jerked once, then went limp. Nash eased him down to the floor, the lifeless weight settling with a dull thud. He stood there for a moment, breathing hard, his gaze flicking toward the window.

The dead man's grey hat lay nearby, knocked loose in the struggle. Nash picked it up, shook off the dust, and settled it on his head. The brim was wide enough to obscure his face from below, and it was a hat those in the street would recognise—just what he needed. He gave the body one last glance before taking up the man's position at the window.

From this height, he had a clear view of the street. Kade's remaining men crouched behind the mine wagon, their weapons ready, but they were exposed now—more than they realized.

Wyatt Steele

Perfect, Nash thought, sliding one of the Colts from its holster.

He rested his elbow on the windowsill, steadying his aim. The lead man peeked out from behind the wagon, scanning the saloon with an angry glare. Nash didn't hesitate.

The Colt barked, the bullet tearing through the man's chest. The impact sent him sprawling back, his rifle clattering onto the dusty ground.

Chaos erupted.

The other men shouted, scrambling for better cover, but the wagon's size worked against them—it was too small to shield all of them. Another man leaned out, frantically searching for Nash's position.

Nash fired again.

This time, the bullet punched into the man's shoulder, spinning him violently before he crashed to the ground, his shout turning into a strangled cry.

That was enough.

The remaining men bolted. One of them grabbed at his fallen comrade, dragging him back by the arm, but the others didn't wait. They turned and ran, sprinting for their horses still hitched further down the street.

Nash watched, his jaw tight as the wagon emptied. He holstered one Colt, keeping the other ready as the last of Kade's men disappeared into the dust cloud they'd kicked up.

Just as he'd hoped, fear had taken hold.

CHAPTER TEN

From his perch, Nash watched the street for a moment longer. Silence settled again. Slowly, Nash pulled back from the window, his shoulders sagging slightly with relief.

"Nash!"

He turned to see Sadie standing in the doorway, her face pale but triumphant. "They're gone! You did it!"

Nash didn't answer at first, the grey hat still shadowing his face, Sadie moved toward him, her eyes bright.

"They're runnin', Nash! You chased 'em off!"

Nash exhaled through his nose, his expression hard. "For now." He turned his head slightly, as if listening for the sound of distant hoofbeats. "But they'll be back. And next time, they'll bring more."

Sadie's face fell, her excitement dampened. "Then what do we do?"

Nash removed the grey hat, tossing it aside as if it carried the weight of what he'd done. "We get ready," he said flatly.

From across the room, Caleb appeared, his face still flushed from the fight. "They're gone for good, though, right? I mean... you got five of 'em."

Nash shook his head, holstering his Colts. "They'll need time to lick their wounds, but Kade doesn't give up that easy."

Sadie looked at him, concern etching her features. "Then what's next?"

"I'm not sure yet," Nash said slowly.

The morning after the gunfire had driven Kade's men back, Blackrock was far from calm. The dusty streets were eerily silent, as if the town itself held its breath, waiting for the storm to break. Smoke still lingered faintly in the air from the night before, a grim reminder of how close Kade's men had come.

Nash stood at the center of the saloon, surrounded by the grim faces of Caleb, Sadie, Jenkins, and the handful of others who'd found the courage—or desperation—to join them. His expression was carved from stone, and every line on his face was set with focus and weariness. A half-empty whiskey bottle sat on the bar, but he hadn't touched it since sunrise.

"We don't have much time," Nash began, his voice carrying to the far corners of the saloon. "Kade's not the kind of man to lick his wounds and walk away. He'll be back, and he'll bring hell with him."

Wyatt Steele

Sadie leaned against the bar, a shotgun resting within arm's reach. She said nothing, her face pale but resolute.

"What do we do, Nash?" Caleb asked. His voice held an edge of uncertainty, but he stood tall. "How do we fight him?"

Nash shifted his weight, looking around at the motley group of defenders. "We dig in. Fortify what we can and hold as long as we're able." He moved to the window and pushed back the curtain. Outside, the town looked even smaller than usual—vulnerable in its isolation. "We don't have the numbers to go to them, so we make Kade's men come to us. And when they do, we make them pay for every step."

"Barricades?" Jenkins rasped from his spot near the door. The old miner was leaning on a shovel like it was a crutch, but his eyes were sharp.

Nash nodded. "Yeah. I want the main street choked up. We'll use whatever we've got—wagons, barrels, planks—anything that slows them down and keeps them from swarming us at once."

Sadie pushed off the bar, crossing her arms. "The saloon's solid enough, and the back doors are barred. We need to watch the balconies again, that's how they got in last time."

"I agree, we'll do a better job of sealing off the stairs," Nash replied.

"And the other buildings?" Caleb asked, his brows knitting together.

Nash exhaled slowly. "Too many to defend. They'll try to use the rooftops. We keep men on watch. If they get close, we deal with it fast. The key is keeping their numbers thin. A few down quick enough, and the rest might lose their nerve." His voice dropped lower, gruff. "We don't win this fight by outlasting 'em. We win it by making them bleed."

The group fell quiet for a moment. Outside, the creak of a sign in the wind sounded louder than it should've, the silence of the town pressing in around them like a weight.

"Do you really think we've got a chance?" Sadie asked, her voice low.

Nash turned, his gaze meeting hers. "I think we've got a choice. We can lay down and let Kade own this town forever, or we can make him work damn hard for it." He paused, his tone softening. "It won't be easy. It'll get ugly, and some of us might not make it. But standing here, doing nothing? That's a sure way to lose."

Jenkins grunted in agreement. "Better to die with a gun in your hand than on your knees."

Sadie looked from Jenkins to Nash, her jaw tightening. "Then let's get to it."

The saloon became a hive of activity. Caleb and his men hammered boards across the saloon's back door while Nash and Jenkins began dragging tables to block the staircase leading to the upper floor. Dust and sweat hung heavy in the air as boots thudded across the wood, every piece of furniture repurposed into a barrier. The front of the saloon had been left a splintered mess, and this was reinforced with thick planking, the windows boarded up and the only light coming into the interior now came in over the top and from under the batwing doors.

Sadie emerged from behind the bar carrying two crates of shotgun shells, setting them on one of the tables Nash had lined up. "If they get close, I'll be ready for 'em," she said, her voice steady. The shotgun never left her side.

Nash inspected the barricade on the stairs, pushing against the tables to ensure they held firm. He glanced at Sadie, a flicker of approval in his eyes. "Good."

Out on the main street, Caleb directed the placement of wagons and barrels, forcing any would-be attackers into a narrow bottleneck. Two young miners worked beside him, sweat pouring down their faces as they hauled planks and crates into place.

By the time the afternoon sun began to dip toward the horizon, Blackrock no longer looked like a defenseless town. Barricades blocked the saloon and choked the streets. Windows had been covered, and rifles waited, propped against walls like silent sentinels.

Nash stood at the saloon door, the Henry rifle slung over his shoulder as he scanned the darkening horizon. The quiet was unnerving, the calm before the storm. His hand twitched at his side, instinctively brushing against the grip of his Colt.

Sadie came up beside him, her voice low. "They're coming, aren't they?"

"Soon," Nash replied, his tone flat.

"And if they don't turn back?"

Nash's eyes narrowed against the dying light. "Then we give 'em hell."

That afternoon, the heat sat heavy over Blackrock, the stillness of the air broken only by the occasional creak of wood or distant hammering as the townsfolk worked to fortify what they could. Dust swirled lazily through the narrow street, catching the harsh light of the sun.

The distant thud of hooves cut through the quiet like a knife.

Nash was the first to step onto the saloon's porch, his gaze narrowing as a lone rider emerged from the horizon, a dark silhouette against the shimmering heatwaves. The man rode slowly, almost deliberately, his horse's pace unhurried as it approached the heart of town. Behind him, trailing in the dirt, a limp figure dragged along by a length of rope tied to the saddle horn.

"Son of a bitch," Nash muttered under his breath, his jaw tightening.

The rider's face came into focus as he neared—cold and emotionless beneath the brim of his black hat. Dust caked his clothing, and a cruel smirk tugged at his lips as he surveyed the town. He was one of Kade's men, no question about it, the kind of man who looked comfortable with violence.

"Get Caleb," Nash said quietly, his voice low but firm. Sadie, who had appeared beside him, nodded and slipped back into the saloon. Nash stepped down off the porch, his hand resting lightly on the butt of his Colt as he moved to the center of the street.

The rider didn't stop until he was close enough for Nash to see the blood staining the dirt where the man's boots dragged. The miner—one of the older hands, gray-bearded and gaunt—was crumpled and unmoving, his face battered beyond recognition. A low murmur rippled through the handful of people who had dared to come out and watch.

The rider leaned lazily in his saddle, his eyes meeting Nash's without a flicker of concern. He yanked the rope free with a careless motion and slung it to the ground.

"Message from Mr. Kade," the rider drawled, his voice dripping with smug satisfaction. "Tomorrow at sundown, Blackrock belongs to him. No more warnings." He paused, letting the words settle over the stunned crowd like a shroud. "You want to fight? You'll end up just like this poor bastard here. And before you think of firing a few shots at me we got a few more miners back at Kade's place, you shoot me and we'll drag two more into town."

Nash said nothing, his face carved from stone, but his hand itched to pull the Colt and put a bullet through the rider's calm façade. Instead, he locked eyes with the man, letting him see the fire burning behind his quiet gaze.

The rider's smirk widened, as if daring Nash to try something. "Pass the word," he said before turning his horse. With a casual tug on the reins, he wheeled around and rode back the way he'd come, the rhythmic clop of hooves echoing off the buildings, slow and deliberate.

For a long moment, no one moved. The crowd stood frozen, staring at the broken man left behind in the dirt, their faces pale with shock and fear. The only sound was the wind stirring through the narrow streets and the faint jingle of the rider's spurs as he faded into the distance.

Nash turned away from the departing figure and knelt beside the miner, checking for any sign of life. There was none. The man's body was broken and lifeless, his sacrifice clear.

Sadie appeared again, Caleb just behind her. Caleb froze, his face draining of color as he recognized the miner. "That's Tom," he whispered hoarsely. "He worked the north shaft." His fists clenched, shaking with barely contained fury. "They didn't have to—"

"They didn't have to, but they did," Nash said flatly, standing and dusting off his hands. His gaze hardened, sweeping over the townsfolk who lingered in the shadows, their expressions stricken. "They wanted you to see this. They wanted you scared."

"And it's working," Sadie muttered, her voice unsteady as her gaze flickered to Tom's body.

Nash didn't argue; he knew she was right. Kade's men were turning the screws, pushing hard to break what little resistance the town had left. Tomorrow at sundown, the blood would flow. Either the town would stand its ground, or it would crumble beneath Kade's heel.

Caleb took a shaky breath, his eyes on Nash. "What do we do?"

Nash's reply was quiet, but there was no hesitation. "We bury Tom."

He glanced back to the horizon, where the rider had disappeared, then to the people of Blackrock, who had begun to gather, whispering amongst themselves. Their fear was palpable, thick in the air like smoke after a fire.

> "We bury him," Nash repeated, his tone iron-hard. "And then we get ready. If Kade wants Blackrock, we'll make sure he pays dearly for it."

CHAPTER ELEVEN

The mood in Blackrock turned quickly after the rider left. The townsfolk gathered in small clusters along the dusty streets, their voices low and urgent, punctuated by sharp whispers and nervous glances toward the horizon. Panic spread like wildfire, a palpable unease crackling through the air as the grim message sank in: Kade was coming.

Nash stood on the saloon porch, his gaze scanning the growing crowd. People were pleading, shouting, their faces drawn and pale. A miner's wife gripped her husband's arm, tears streaking her dusty cheeks as she begged him to leave town. An older man, shoulders stooped and hands trembling, muttered to anyone who would listen that they'd all be dead by sundown tomorrow.

"We can't win!" a voice shouted from the throng. "There's too many of 'em. We're not fighters!"

"Better to pack up what we can and leave!" another added, a chorus of agreements rippling outward.

Nash pushed off the railing and descended the steps, his boots thudding heavily on the hard-packed ground. "Running's not going to save you," he called, his voice cutting through the chaos. The murmurs quieted slightly as heads turned his way. "Kade's men aren't gonna stop at the town limits. You give him Blackrock, you give him everything. He'll hunt you down wherever you go, just to make sure you don't get back up."

A few pairs of eyes locked on Nash, their expressions uncertain, torn between fear and fleeting hope. But the panic still simmered beneath the surface, ready to boil over. Nash could feel it like a weight in the air.

"And what are we supposed to do?" a burly miner demanded, stepping forward. "You said it yourself, Kade's got more men, more guns. We ain't soldiers!"

Nash's jaw tightened. He wanted to snap back, to say that not being soldiers didn't matter, that standing their ground was their only chance. But his own doubt gnawed at him, its voice whispering louder than the miners'. You're asking them to die. You know it. They'll never survive this.

"Maybe he's right," someone else muttered from the back of the crowd.

For a moment, Nash's eyes flickered—just a moment of hesitation, but long enough for Sadie to see it. She stood near the saloon doors, arms crossed tightly, her gaze drilling into him.

"That's enough!" Sadie's voice rang out, sharp as a whip crack. She stepped down into the street, her boots kicking up little puffs of dust as she marched toward Nash. "We've got more fight in us than you're giving us credit for!" she shot at the crowd. Then she turned on Nash, her eyes blazing.

Nash's expression darkened as he looked at her. "Don't start this, Sadie."

"Why not?" she snapped, her voice rising. "You're the one standing here, telling us to fight, but you don't even believe we can win. You think they can't see that?" She gestured at the townsfolk, her words like sparks in the dry wind. "People aren't stupid, Nash. They know when someone's lost their nerve."

Nash stepped closer, his voice low and tight. "You think this is about nerves? About me? I'm trying to keep these people alive."

Sadie's hands balled into fists at her sides. "Are you? Or are you just afraid to lose again?"

The accusation hit like a hammer, and for a moment, Nash couldn't breathe. The street seemed to grow quieter around them, the words hanging heavy in the air. He stared at her, anger flaring to mask the truth that her words cut too close to.

"You don't know what you're talking about," he growled.

Sadie didn't back down. She stepped right up to him, her chin tilted defiantly. "Don't I? You're fighting more than Kade, Nash. You're fighting yourself, and it's killing you." She gestured to the people watching them—fearful, desperate people who wanted nothing more than a reason to believe they could survive this. "They need you, damn it. But all they're getting is a man too busy wrestling with ghosts to see what's right in front of him."

Nash's mouth tightened into a hard line, his face a mask of barely contained anger. "You think I want this? You think I want to be here at all? If I'd done the smart thing, I'd have been long gone."

"Then why are you still here?" Sadie demanded, her voice quieter now, but no less intense. "If you're so ready to walk away, why are you still standing here, telling them to fight? You could've ridden out days ago."

Nash stared at her, his breathing hard, his mind warring with itself. Because she was right. He didn't know why he hadn't left—why he hadn't taken the easy way out. Something kept pulling him back, something he didn't have a name for. Guilt, duty, or maybe just that infuriating woman standing in front of him now.

Sadie shook her head, her voice softening. "You care, Nash. Whether you like it or not, you care. And if you're going to stand here and tell us to fight, then fight with us—believe in us."

He swallowed hard, unable to look at her for a moment. Instead, he turned his eyes to the crowd, to the faces of men and women who still looked at him with doubt, but also with the faintest flicker of hope. His shoulders squared.

"We've got one night," Nash said finally, his voice steady, resolute. "One night to get ready, and one night to decide what we stand for. I'm not gonna lie to you—it's going to be hard, and not everyone's walking out of this alive. But if you want to stop Kade, it starts now."

The crowd was silent. Then, slowly, Caleb stepped forward. "I'll fight," he said, his voice cracking but firm.

A few others murmured in agreement, some of the doubt beginning to lift.
Sadie glanced back at Nash, the fire still in her eyes, but something softer there too. She held his gaze for a moment before turning to the townsfolk. "Start gathering whatever you can—guns, ammunition, tools. If you can hold a hammer, a pitchfork, or a damn spoon, you're helping fortify this town."

The townspeople dispersed, a new energy in their steps, though the fear still lingered. Nash exhaled slowly, running a hand through his hair, his expression grim. He glanced at Sadie, who stood nearby watching him.

"Damn woman," he muttered under his breath. She smirked faintly, but neither of them spoke further. There was too much work to do—and not enough time to do it.

The night air was cooler than it had been all day, a welcome reprieve from the unrelenting heat. Nash stood on the saloon's balcony, hands resting on the worn wooden railing as he stared

Wyatt Steele

out over Blackrock. The town lay quiet and still, but there was no peace in it—just the heavy hush of people waiting for what tomorrow would bring. Lamps glowed dimly behind curtained windows, silhouettes passing by as families prepared for what might be their last night together.

Above it all, the stars shone down, cold and indifferent. Nash had spent enough nights under open skies to know that the world didn't give a damn about the lives of men. People fought, they died, and the stars still burned as if nothing had happened at all.

He reached for the bottle of whiskey beside him, taking a long pull before setting it back down with a dull thud. The familiar burn settled in his chest, but it didn't chase away the weight pressing down on him—the weight he'd carried for far too long.

Emily.

Her name drifted through his mind like a ghost, as unwelcome as it was familiar. Nash closed his eyes for a moment, and there she was: standing by the ranch house, sunlight catching in her hair, laughing at something he'd said. The sound of her voice, soft and warm, tugged at something deep inside him, a place he thought he'd buried long ago.

She'd believed in him—damn her, she had believed in him. And he had let her down, just like he'd let so many others down before her. She'd been the best part of him, and he'd lost her. Two years had passed, and the ache was still sharp enough to cut through bone.

His thoughts drifted to Sadie, and his grip on the railing tightened. He didn't want to think about her—didn't want to remember the softness of her in his arms, the way she'd looked at him with both fire and understanding. It wasn't supposed to happen. She wasn't supposed to get under his skin.

But she had.

Damn the woman, she'd managed it all right.

Her laughter, her temper, the way she stood up to him when no one else dared—it stirred something in him that he couldn't name. And that terrified him more than anything Kade and his men could throw at him. He didn't know if it was because he missed Emily or if it was something deeper, something he didn't want to admit to himself.

He lifted the whiskey bottle again, but this time, he just stared at it. For a brief moment, he thought about going back inside, finding Sadie, and telling her everything—how he didn't know if he was fighting for this town or for her, how he didn't know if he had it in him to survive losing something again.

But he didn't move.

Instead, Nash set the bottle down with a deliberate calm and let his gaze sweep over the town once more. Blackrock looked fragile under the moonlight like a single gust of wind might shatter it. Tomorrow, Kade would come, and men would die. Nash didn't know if he could stop it. But for whatever reason—whether it was because of Sadie, Caleb, or the ghost of Emily that wouldn't let him be—he knew he'd fight.

"Coward," he muttered to himself, shaking his head. That was what Sadie had called him earlier, and maybe she wasn't wrong. Maybe he was a coward. But he was a coward who'd stand his ground tomorrow, even if it killed him.

The wind picked up, whistling softly through the empty streets below. Nash stood there for a long time, watching, waiting—haunted by memories and weighed down by the knowledge that, come tomorrow, everything might burn.

CHAPTER TWELVE

The saloon was silent except for the low creak of chairs and the shuffling of feet as Nash stood at the center, a rough map of Blackrock sketched across one of the saloon's tables. Around him, Caleb, Sadie, Jack, and a handful of miners and townsfolk leaned in, their faces tight with tension and fear. The lamplight cast long shadows on the walls, making the room feel smaller, the weight of what was to come pressing down on everyone like a stone.

Nash planted his hands on the table, his voice low but steady, the kind that commanded attention. "Listen up. We're outnumbered, outgunned, and we don't have the luxury of a second chance. If Kade's men come at sundown, they'll hit us hard, and we're not gonna beat 'em by standing out in the open. We've got to make 'em fight for every damn inch."

He took a piece of chalk and drew an 'X' over the saloon on the map. "The saloon's the strongest position we've got—it's where we'll make our stand. From here, we can cover the main street and give Kade's boys a proper welcome. Caleb, you and Jake will hold the front. Stack the tables and barrels up against the windows. They'll try to come through the doors, so you keep those shotguns ready."

Caleb grunted, nodding his agreement. "They'll have to blow the doors off their hinges to get through."

"Exactly," Nash said, tapping the chalk against the table. "Next, we need eyes and rifles on the rooftops." He looked up at Jake. "You, Ket, and a few others get up there with whatever guns you've got. From the roofs, you'll have a clear shot on anyone coming up the street."

Jake swallowed hard, his brow furrowed, but he nodded. "We'll cover you. Promise."

"Good," Nash replied, his voice firm. "Stay low and move slow. Don't give Kade's men an easy target." He marked two narrow alleys leading to the saloon. "Now, these two choke points are the next thing we hold. Kade's men are smart enough to look for side entrances when the front stalls. We barricade them. Two men at each, with pistols and shotguns. If anyone tries to push through, you make 'em regret it."

A murmur of uneasy agreement ran through the group. Sadie, leaning against the bar with her arms crossed, watched Nash intently, her sharp gaze never leaving his face. She spoke up, her voice calm but pointed. "And what about the rear of the saloon? If they get past us, they'll flank you."

Nash turned to her and nodded. "Already thought of that. The back doors are gonna be barred tight. Anyone not assigned to the front or the choke points will take positions there with orders to shoot anything that tries to climb in or break through. Don't hesitate—if you see a shadow, you pull the trigger."

"What about their wagons or horses?" one of the miners asked nervously. "If they bring cover, like they did earlier, they'll get too close."

Nash's jaw tightened, his gaze shifting to the men gathered around. "If they roll another wagon in, we burn it before it gets close. I'll set it myself if I have to." The room went quiet at that, and Nash let the silence stretch for a moment, knowing the weight of his words. "This fight ain't gonna be clean, and it sure as hell won't be fair. If you think you can't pull the trigger, now's the time to walk away."

No one moved. Faces lined with grime and exhaustion stared back at him, hardened by years of struggle, but there was determination in their eyes, too—enough that Nash knew they weren't turning back.

Caleb broke the silence. "What about when they come at us full force? All thirty of them?"

Nash looked straight at him, his voice quieter now, though no less firm. "We're not fighting to kill every last one of them. We're fighting to break 'em. We hit 'em hard, hit 'em fast, and make 'em think twice. Men like Kade, they rely on fear. Take that away, and you take away their strength."

Sadie pushed away from the bar, stepping forward. "You think we can win?"

Nash glanced at her, then back at the map. "We don't need to win outright. If we can make Kade's men pay too high a price, they'll scatter. Men don't die for a cause like his—they die because they think they can't get out of it. If we're smart, we'll give 'em every reason to run."

The room was heavy with tension as Nash straightened, the sound of his boots on the wooden floor loud in the silence. "Get your guns, get your ammunition. Barricade what needs barricading. And get some rest while you can." His gaze moved over each of them, his face set like stone. "Today's gonna be long."

The men began to disperse, talking quietly among themselves as they prepared. Caleb grabbed a handful of miners, already planning who would take the rooftops. Sadie lingered a moment, watching Nash with that same unreadable expression.

"You've got them believing, Nash," she said quietly.

He turned to her, his mouth pulling into a grim line. "Belief's a dangerous thing."

"And why's that?"

"Because it gets people killed," he replied flatly.

Revenge of the Gunfighter

Sadie didn't say anything, but as she turned and walked away, Nash couldn't help but feel the weight of her eyes on him. He looked back at the map one last time, his fingers resting on the marked saloon. Tomorrow, men would die, maybe all of them. But if they were lucky, they'd take the fight out of Kade for good.

That was all they could hope for now.

The late afternoon sun cast long shadows over the dusty street as Nash adjusted the barricade near the saloon's batwing doors, double-checking the positions of the makeshift cover. The town was quiet—too quiet. It felt like the air itself was holding its breath, waiting for the storm to hit.

Nash paused, squinting down the main road toward the shimmering horizon. He froze when he saw them—figures moving through the heat waves, kicking up dust as they came closer. For a heartbeat, his hand hovered near his Colt, the instinct to draw and defend kicking in hard, but something about their gait told him this wasn't Kade's men.

From behind him, Sadie stepped onto the saloon's porch, her shotgun in hand. She followed his gaze, her expression tensing. "Who the hell is that?"

The figures grew clearer as they approached—a ragged band of men, some on foot, others on tired-looking horses. At the front of the group, an old man limped along with the help of a sturdy walking stick, his long shadow dragging across the dirt.

"Jenkins," Nash muttered under his breath, both surprised and wary.

By the time they reached the saloon, the group had gathered a small cloud of onlookers, the townsfolk emerging cautiously from behind shutters and doors to see what was happening. The old miner came to a stop in front of Nash, his weathered face cracked into a stubborn grin.

"You look like you've seen a ghost," Jenkins wheezed, leaning heavily on his stick. His clothes were dusty, his hat crooked on his head, and his boots looked like they'd been on the trail longer than they should have. Behind him, a half-dozen other men—gray-haired, scarred, and rough as uncut stone—stood with shotguns, old rifles, and pistols hanging from their hips.

"Jenkins," Nash said, stepping off the porch.

The old man straightened as much as his bad leg would allow, a glint of defiance in his eyes. "Heard tell that Kade's comin' for Blackrock. Heard you were the one standin' against him."

Nash didn't say anything, his eyes scanning the group of men. Retired miners, cowhands with shaky knees, a couple who looked like they'd barely held a rifle in years. It wasn't much, but they were here, and they'd come willing.

"Ain't right to let you fight this one alone." He turned slightly, gesturing to the ragged men behind him. "We all got our reasons. We may be old, but we've got enough left in us to shoot straight."

Nash looked at the group, his mouth pulling into a thin line. He wanted to tell them to turn around, to get the hell out while they still could. But when he looked at Jenkins—at the raw determination in the old man's face—he knew it wouldn't matter what he said.

"This fight's gonna get ugly," Nash said finally, his tone grave. "Kade won't hold back."

Jenkins barked a hoarse laugh. "Son, we've been fightin' our whole lives. Mines, landowners, bad luck—you name it. Ain't a single one of us afraid of dyin', but I'll be damned if I let Kade burn this town to the ground without a fight."

Behind Nash, Sadie's expression softened as she took in the sight of the old men, their tired but unyielding stances. Caleb, standing off to the side with Ket and Jake, looked both stunned and relieved.

"Well," Nash said, nodding slowly, "if you're set on staying, I'll make sure you've got something to do." He turned back toward the saloon, beckoning for Caleb. "Get 'em set up. Extra ammo's in the saloon. Put a couple on the choke points and the rest on the rooftops. You know what to do."

Caleb grinned, his confidence returning now that they had more men on their side. "You got it, Nash."

As the group dispersed, Jenkins stepped closer, his voice dropping to a gruff murmur. "I don't reckon we're gonna turn the tide single-handed, but maybe we'll make 'em think twice."

Nash gave him a long, appraising look before clapping the old man gently on the shoulder. "Just stay alive long enough to get a few shots off, Jenkins."

Jenkins grinned through cracked lips. "Hell, Nash. I aim to shoot first and die later."

Nash couldn't help but chuckle under his breath as he watched Jenkins limp off toward the saloon. The old man's presence, ragged and unexpected as it was, had done something no plan of his could—it had given the defenders hope.

Sadie stepped up beside Nash, watching the group of newcomers move into position. "They're not much," she said softly, her voice somewhere between admiration and worry.

"No," Nash replied, his eyes still on Jenkins. "But they're enough."

The saloon was a hum of quiet activity as the defenders prepared for what was coming. Nash stood at the bar, double-checking his Colts, each click of the cylinder echoing in the tense silence. The Henry rifle leaned against the counter within arm's reach, and his face was set like stone—focused, unreadable.

Sadie's voice broke the quiet. "You're not leaving me out of this."

Nash didn't look up. "I already told you, Sadie. You're stayin' out of the way." He slipped a final round into the Colt and snapped it shut, the motion crisp and decisive.

Sadie stepped toward him, hands on her hips, her chin tilted stubbornly. "Kade's taken my town, burned my saloon, and pushed my people to the brink. I don't need you telling me what fight is mine and what isn't."

Nash finally raised his eyes to meet hers. The defiance in her face was familiar—too familiar. He'd seen it in Emily before, and the memory stung more than he cared to admit. "Sadie," he said, his voice low but firm, "I don't need you dyin' to prove a point."

Sadie's lips tightened. "You think I don't know what this is? That I'm not scared?" She stepped closer, her voice trembling, though her resolve didn't waver. "I *am* scared, Nash. I'm scared of what Kade will do if we don't stop him. I'm scared of what'll happen to Caleb, to Jenkins, to this whole town. And yeah, I'm scared I won't make it out of this alive. But I'll be damned if I'm gonna sit in a corner and wait for someone else to fight my battle for me."

Nash stared at her, taking in the fire in her eyes, the set of her jaw. Her words hung between them, raw and unflinching. He couldn't deny the truth in them, and it annoyed him off because deep down, he knew she wasn't going to back down.

"You're makin' this harder than it needs to be," Nash muttered, running a hand through his hair. "You don't need to—"

"I *do* need to," Sadie interrupted. Her voice softened then, her eyes searching his face. "I'm not going anywhere."

For a long moment, Nash said nothing. His eyes lingered on her face, seeing the fear there but also the determination that outshone it. He swallowed hard, his throat tight with emotions he didn't want to name. It was that damned woman again, making it harder to keep himself detached—harder to pretend he didn't care.

"Fine," he said finally, his voice rough. "But you stay close to me. You don't take any chances, and you don't go playin' hero." His gaze locked onto hers, hard and unyielding. "If I tell you to move, you move. If I tell you to shoot, you shoot. Got it?"

Sadie nodded, her eyes glistening faintly in the low light. "Got it."

Nash let out a slow breath, his jaw clenched as he reached for the Henry rifle. "You're a damn fool, Sadie," he muttered, though the edge had softened from his voice.

Sadie managed a small smile, one that didn't quite erase the fear in her eyes. "Takes one to know one, cowboy."

He shook his head, unable to stop the faintest tug at the corner of his mouth. Damn her for making him care. He handed her a loaded shotgun from behind the bar, his hands lingering just a moment too long as he passed it to her. "Stick close," he said again, more softly this time. "I mean it."

Sadie nodded, her fingers tightening on the weapon. "I will."

For just a heartbeat, they stood there, the world beyond the saloon forgotten. Nash stared at her—this stubborn, infuriating woman who somehow managed to find a way past his defenses. There were things he wanted to say, things he couldn't bring himself to admit. Instead, he reached out and touched her arm, his thumb brushing against the fabric of her sleeve.

"We make 'em pay, Sadie," he murmured, his voice low and steady. "For everything."

Sadie's smile faltered, replaced by something softer, more vulnerable. "For everything," she echoed.

Nash turned away before the moment could stretch any further, grabbing his rifle and striding toward the door. "Let's get ready," he said gruffly. "They'll be comin' soon."

Sadie followed him, her shotgun clutched tight, her steps steady. Outside, the wind had picked up, carrying with it the scent of dust and smoke—a promise of the battle to come.

Wyatt Steele

As dusk fell, Blackrock sank into an uneasy stillness. The last rays of sunlight bled red across the horizon, stretching long shadows down the main street like dark fingers grasping for something just out of reach. The town was a hushed shell, its people hidden away, bracing for the storm that was sure to come.

Nash walked the empty street, his boots stirring dust with each slow, deliberate step. He moved like a man carrying the weight of inevitability—checking positions, eyeing the makeshift barricades, and nodding to the few defenders as he passed. Their faces were drawn tight, etched with fear and resolve. Each one of them knew the truth: this might be the last night they'd see. Nash knew it too.

He moved without words, his rifle slung across his back, the weight of his Colts a familiar comfort at his hips. Caleb and the two miners sat crouched near the saloon, rifles ready and hands trembling slightly. Jenkins and his men were stationed further down by the old hardware store, their silhouettes dark against the fading light. Nash didn't linger long with any of them. He just checked, gave a silent nod, and moved on.

At last, he reached the stables at the far end of town. The scent of hay and horses drifted to him as he pushed through the wooden doors, his footsteps echoing faintly in the quiet gloom. A lantern hung from a hook, casting pools of golden light onto the rough-hewn walls.

Revenge of the Gunfighter

His mare stood in her stall, her dark coat catching the soft glow. She lifted her head as Nash approached, ears pricking forward, the sound of his low, familiar voice carrying softly in the stillness.

"Hey there, girl," he murmured, running a calloused hand down her neck. She huffed, leaning into his touch, the quiet sound stirring something deep in his chest. "How're you holdin' up?"

The mare blinked at him, her steady gaze offering no judgment, no questions—just the quiet, unspoken bond of trust they'd carried through so many miles. Nash exhaled a slow breath, leaning his forehead briefly against her flank as if drawing strength from the steady rhythm of her breathing.

He reached into his vest pocket and pulled out a small sugar cube he'd been saving. Holding it out on his palm, he let her lips brush against his hand as she took the treat, chewing softly. The noise was comforting, grounding.

He turned and leaned back against the stall door, staring at nothing for a moment as the lantern light swayed. Outside, the last shreds of daylight were fading, and the night—along with all it promised—was settling in.

Nash pushed off the door and gave his mare one last pat, brushing her mane gently from her eyes. "Rest easy, girl," he murmured. "One way or another, we're gettin' through this."

Wyatt Steele

The stables fell silent again as he turned and walked out, his silhouette cutting against the twilight. Behind him, the mare watched him go, her dark eyes following him until the door swung shut, leaving only the echo of his steps.

CHAPTER THIRTEEN

Every window in Blackrock was shuttered, every door bolted tight. Somewhere in the distance, a coyote howled, the lonely cry quickly swallowed by the oppressive silence.

Then, faint at first, came the unmistakable sound of hooves—a slow, measured cadence that grew louder with each passing second. Nash stood just inside the saloon, his silhouette framed by the flickering lamplight, the Henry rifle cradled in his hands. Beside him, Sadie gripped her shotgun, her jaw tight, her knuckles white.

From his position, Nash peered out through the narrow crack between the batwing doors. They came like a black tide, their horses kicking up the dust in slow, deliberate waves. At the head of the column rode Elijah Kade, perched atop a coal-black stallion, his figure cutting a sharp, menacing silhouette against the dying glow of the sky. He wore a long, dust-streaked coat that seemed to move with the wind, and his wide-brimmed hat cast his face in shadow, save for the gleam of his cold, predatory eyes.

Behind him, nearly thirty men fanned out into a line as they reached the center of town. The sharp ring of metal echoed as a dozen torches were struck and set ablaze, their orange flames licking upward like tongues of hellfire. The light cast long, twisting shadows across the street, and for a moment, it seemed as though Blackrock itself had descended into some infernal place.

Nash's jaw clenched as he watched Kade reign in his horse. The stallion pawed at the ground, the sound of its snorting breath audible even from a distance. Kade's men sat astride their mounts with the casual arrogance of wolves at a slaughter, torches in one hand, guns at the ready in the other.

Kade shifted in his saddle and surveyed the town. He let the silence stretch, as if savoring the fear that hung in the air. Then his voice rang out, deep and taunting, carrying with it an edge of lethal calm.

"People of Blackrock!" he called, his words echoing off the wooden walls of the buildings. "I've come to give you one final chance."

Nash could hear the strain in Sadie's breathing beside him, but he kept his gaze fixed on the street. Kade's words were slow, deliberate, spoken with the confidence of a man who believed himself untouchable.

"You know why I'm here," Kade continued, his voice dripping with menace. "You've got yourselves all stirred up, all full of false hope. Hope's a dangerous thing. It'll get you killed."

He leaned forward in his saddle, his eyes narrowing as he scanned the saloon, the sheriff's office, and the barricades that had been thrown together with scraps of furniture and crates. "Give me what I want," Kade said, his tone dropping to a growl, "and I'll let you all live. Put your guns down, walk out, and Blackrock might just survive the night."

He waited, his horse shifting beneath him, its dark flanks rippling with muscle. Kade's men grinned from their positions, flames reflecting in their eyes, eager for the violence they hoped would follow.

No one answered. The town remained still.

Kade's smirk widened. "No? Not one soul brave enough to speak?" He clicked his tongue, shaking his head as though disappointed. "Fine, then. When this night is over, there won't be a damned building left standing, and you'll have no one to blame but yourselves."

From his place in the saloon, Nash let out a slow breath, steadying himself. The words rattled like iron chains in his ears, but he'd expected no less. Kade wasn't a man to bluff. He meant every word.

"They're gonna burn us out," Sadie whispered, her voice barely audible over the crackling torches and the creak of leather saddles. She looked at Nash, her face pale in the flickering light.

Nash didn't look back. His gaze remained fixed on Kade as he sat like a dark king in the street, the flames of his men's torches casting ominous patterns that danced across the buildings.

"Let 'em try," Nash said quietly, his voice like steel. He turned to Sadie for the briefest moment, and their eyes met. "Get ready."

Outside, Kade lifted a hand, signaling to his men. The torches were held higher, their light gleaming off gun barrels and grinning teeth.

The storm had arrived.

Nash watched from the shadows of the saloon, his face carved from stone as Kade's men moved into position. The torches flared, their light reflecting off gun barrels and cruel grins, the smell of kerosene and smoke beginning to seep into the cool evening air. From his spot behind the barricade, Caleb crouched low, his rifle braced against the shattered window frame. His breathing was quick and sharp, his finger tense on the trigger.

Nash's voice came low and steady, a whisper in the dark. *"Now."*

Caleb didn't hesitate. The crack of his rifle split the night like a thunderclap. One of Kade's men, a wiry figure carrying a torch, stumbled backward with a yell, his arms flailing as he dropped into the dust, the torch rolling from his limp hand. Chaos followed.

"Gunfire!" someone shouted, the voice panicked and raw. The remaining torches wavered, their flames jagged in the rising frenzy. Kade's men ducked low, some firing blindly toward the barricades, while others scrambled to find cover in the growing darkness.

"Keep shooting!" Nash barked, his own Henry rifle finding a target. More shots rang out, and another man toppled from his horse, the animal whinnying and rearing as its rider hit the ground.

The street exploded into chaos. Kade's men shouted orders, their voices clashing with the deafening sound of gunfire. Bullets splintered wood and shattered windows as they slammed into buildings, sending shards flying. A sharp *crack* ricocheted off the saloon walls, and Sadie flinched as a bullet tore through the air above her head.

"They're flanking!" Caleb yelled, ducking down as another round of shots hammered the barricade. The dust churned beneath the boots of Kade's men as they surged forward, moving in short, chaotic bursts, using the flickering torchlight to navigate the maze of Blackrock's narrow street.

From further down, Nash's worst fear sparked to life. One of Kade's men broke off from the main group, a torch held high as he sprinted toward the general store. Nash's gut twisted as he saw the man hurl the flame through the shop's front window.

Glass shattered. Flames bloomed inside like a living thing, crawling hungrily across the wooden shelves. Smoke billowed, black and heavy, rolling into the street. The fire cast eerie, shifting shadows across the buildings, its orange glow painting the chaos in a hellish light.

"Dammit," Nash growled, reloading his Henry with practiced speed. The saloon's front walls rattled under the weight of the assault, bullets thudding into the wooden planks like iron fists.

"They're pushing forward!" Sadie shouted from her position behind the bar, her shotgun primed and ready.

Nash turned his head sharply. "Hold 'em back! They're not getting through!" His voice carried over the sound of shattering glass and the steady rhythm of gunfire, a lifeline of control in the madness.

Another volley erupted from Kade's men, the shots wild and desperate. A bullet hissed past Nash's ear, close enough to leave a whisper of heat. He ducked back behind cover, the Henry tucked tight against his shoulder as he peered through a crack in the barricade.

The flames from the shop crept higher, throwing long, licking tendrils of light against the approaching men. Kade's gang moved like ghosts, shadows against the fire, their silhouettes visible as they darted between cover and fired.

Revenge of the Gunfighter

Nash spotted a figure—a big man with a wide-brimmed hat—trying to drag a water trough into the street for cover. Nash lined up his shot. The Henry barked, and the man fell with a groan, slumping to the dirt.

"Caleb! Ket! Keep their heads down!" Nash roared. Caleb fired again, the flash from his rifle briefly lighting the sweat-drenched determination on his face.

More shouts rose from Kade's men as they slowed, disoriented by the darkness, the fires, and the unrelenting gunfire coming from the saloon. Nash knew they'd bought themselves only a few moments—the tide was pressing, but it hadn't yet broken.

He glanced at Sadie, her eyes fierce as she reloaded with trembling hands. "You hold here, and stay behind the bar," he told her, his voice low but resolute. "Whatever it takes."

Sadie nodded, gripping the shotgun tighter. "I will."

Then, before she could object Nash left the saloon and entered the chaos outside, his jaw set as the fire climbed higher, and the night exploded with gunfire once more. He could do more damage outside.

The night erupted in violence. The steady *crack* of rifles echoed off the buildings, mingling with the shouts of men and the roar of fire. Blackrock, a town used to swallowing its pride, finally fought back.

Wyatt Steele

Miners lay prone on the rooftops, silhouetted against the orange glow of burning buildings. Their rifles kicked back with every shot, and more than one of Kade's men toppled to the dirt below, their bodies jerking like marionettes with cut strings. They were rough shots, these miners, but desperation made up for their lack of skill.

Down in the alleys and behind makeshift barricades of barrels, crates, and broken wagons, others held their ground. Shotguns and pistols thundered, each blast like a challenge hurled into the dark. A miner in a ragged coat crouched behind a stack of firewood, firing an ancient revolver until the cylinder clicked empty. With shaking hands, he reloaded, sweat streaking through the dirt on his face.

Nash moved through it all, a silent, deadly presence. He darted from shadow to shadow, his long coat blending with the darkness. Kade's men barely saw him coming before he struck. One of Kade's enforcers rounded a corner, rifle raised, his breath harsh from the heat of the fire. Before he could pull the trigger, Nash's Colt barked twice, the bullets punching him backward into the dust.

Gun smoke hung in the air, thick and choking, the acrid smell searing Nash's nostrils. He reloaded quickly, ducking behind an overturned wagon as a hail of bullets splintered the wood around him. Sparks flew as stray rounds struck metal. He turned his head and spotted three of Kade's men rushing toward a side alley, trying to flank the saloon.

"Not tonight," Nash muttered.

Sliding out from cover, he lifted the Henry rifle from his back and braced it against his shoulder. His pulse steadied, his breath slowing as he sighted the first man. *Crack.* The man dropped face-first into the dirt.

The second man turned, panic flaring in his eyes as he fumbled with his revolver. Nash squeezed the trigger again. The shot landed square in the middle of his chest, and he crumpled with a thud. The third man froze, half in shadow, before spinning on his heel and bolting. Nash let him run. Fear would do more damage than a bullet.

Overhead, Caleb's voice shouted down from the rooftop. "They're pullin' back toward the street!"

Nash glanced up, catching sight of Caleb's silhouette as he crouched low and fired at another figure moving through the gloom. The boy's aim was getting better, but his voice trembled with the adrenaline of battle.

Nash kept moving, weaving through the alleys like smoke, his guns barking when the opportunity presented itself. He caught two more of Kade's men taking cover behind a water trough, their backs turned as they reloaded. Nash didn't hesitate. His Colt roared, and both men slumped over, blood seeping into the dry earth.

Wyatt Steele

Flames crackled from the shop Kade's men had set ablaze, the fire licking at the darkened sky. The heat was fierce, driving townsfolk further back into their barricades. Nash glanced toward the saloon, where Sadie's shotgun boomed through the night, her figure framed briefly by the firelight as she stood behind an open window. Damn the woman! She'd not stayed behind the bar where he'd told to her stop.

The din of the battle began to shift, Kade's men realizing they were taking losses they hadn't anticipated. Shouts of confusion carried across the street, some of the gang yelling for retreat, others barking orders to keep pushing forward.

Nash knew the tide was turning. He crouched behind an old cart, his chest heaving as he reloaded his weapons, sweat dripping down his face. Across the way, miners and townsfolk began rallying, their spirits rising as they realized Kade's men weren't invincible.

Jake Black, one of Caleb's miner friends, popped up from behind a barrel and yelled, "They're fallin' back! Keep at 'em, boys!"

The defenders let out a ragged cheer, their gunfire intensifying as Kade's men scrambled for cover.

Nash pushed forward, rising from his position and advancing down the street with measured steps, his Colt raised and ready. A wounded enforcer stumbled into view, clutching his bleeding side, but before he could raise his weapon, Nash fired. The man spun and dropped, motionless.

By the time Nash reached the center of the street, the battle had shifted. Kade's men, leaderless and disorganized, were breaking apart. Some sprinted for their horses, others fled into the shadows. A handful remained, firing blindly in desperation as they scrambled for any semblance of cover.

"Push 'em out!" Caleb roared from the rooftop, his voice carrying over the chaos.

And they did. Nash fired his last shot and dropped another man near the water tower before pausing to reload, his hands slick with sweat and gunpowder. Around him, the townsfolk surged forward, their resolve hardening.

The street grew quieter, the gunfire fading as the last of Kade's gang disappeared into the darkness. The defenders didn't cheer this time— they were too tired, too aware that the night wasn't over yet.

Nash stood in the center of the street, the Henry rifle hanging loosely in his grip as he scanned the smoke-filled scene. Bodies littered the ground, flames still flickered from the shopfront, and the acrid smell of blood and gunpowder clung to the air. Then Kade's men's horses hammered back down the street, heading straight to the saloon. Tightening his grip on the rifle, Nash ran back to the saloon calling for the others behind the barricades to join him.

Wyatt Steele

The crash of wood splintering under heavy boots rang out like a thunderclap. Nash spun toward the sound, his eyes narrowing. The barricade over the saloon doors shuddered violently as Kade's men hurled their weight against it, the crude barrier groaning under the assault. Dust sifted down from the ceiling, and the sharp slam of fists and rifle butts echoed through the saloon like a drumbeat of war.

"They're comin' in!" Caleb's voice cracked with panic as he swung his rifle toward the doors, the stock trembling in his grip.

"Hold steady!" Nash barked, his voice cutting through the noise. He reloaded one of his Colts with practiced speed, snapping the chamber shut as another brutal impact shook the barricade. He knew it wouldn't hold—not for much longer.

Sadie was crouched behind the bar, shotgun in hand, her face pale but resolute. "They're gonna come through!" she called over her shoulder.

"I know!" Nash's jaw tightened. "Get ready."

With a final thunderous *crack,* the barricade gave way, the wood exploding inward in a storm of splinters. The batwing doors were kicked aside as Kade's men poured in, shouting and firing wild shots that splintered the saloon's tables and glass. A lantern shattered, flames licking up the edge of the wall.

"Down!" Nash shouted, grabbing Caleb by the collar and dragging him behind an overturned table. Bullets whined past, one slamming into a support beam, another punching through the wood of the bar where Sadie was crouched.

The saloon erupted into chaos.

Nash rose, firing both Colts, their deafening barks filling the room. The first man through the doorway dropped like a stone, a red blossom blooming across his chest. Another charged in after him, wielding a sawed-off shotgun. Nash's next shot caught him in the thigh, sending him sprawling onto the bloodstained floor with a cry of pain.

Behind the bar, Sadie gritted her teeth and stood, her shotgun already at her shoulder. She fired, the weapon's roar shaking the saloon as buckshot tore into two of Kade's rushing through the wreckage. One man crumpled, his weapon clattering to the floor; the other stumbled back, blood pouring from his side as he collapsed into the doorway.

Caleb, his breathing ragged, raised his rifle. He lined up a shot with shaking hands and fired, the recoil knocking him back. A man who'd been climbing through a shattered window fell backward with a strangled cry, his body disappearing into the darkness outside.

Wyatt Steele

Nash ducked as a bullet grazed the edge of the table, splinters peppering his face. His hat flew off, but he didn't stop. In one fluid motion, he emptied the last rounds from his Colts, dropping two more of Kade's men who had dared to advance. One tumbled headfirst into a pile of shattered chairs, while the other fell hard against a table, bringing it crashing down with him.

"Caleb! Reload!" Nash growled, tossing one of his empty Colts aside and pulling the Smith and Wesson from his belt. He fired a round that struck a man in the shoulder, spinning the man around before he crashed into a wall.

Caleb fumbled, sweat streaming down his face. "I'm tryin', I'm tryin'!"

Sadie reloaded with shaking hands, ducking as bullets riddled the bar. "There's too many of 'em!" she shouted, flinching as a mirror behind her shattered into a thousand shards.

Nash reloaded the Smith and Wesson, his movements quick and deadly. "We don't stop!" he barked. "We take 'em down one at a time!"

Another man lunged forward, close enough for Nash to see the whites of his eyes. The man swung a pistol like a club, but Nash ducked under the blow and rammed his shoulder into the man's chest, sending him sprawling. Nash followed up with a hard swing of his revolver, cracking it across the man's skull with a sickening *thud*. The man went limp.

Revenge of the Gunfighter

Nash turned to find two more men charging toward the bar. Sadie stepped out from cover, her teeth bared as she fired the shotgun again. The blast caught one square in the chest, hurling him backward into a support post. The second man hesitated, shocked at the carnage, and Nash took his shot. The bullet hit home, and the man folded to the ground.

"Damn it!" Nash hissed as he reloaded, his hands slick with sweat and grime. He stole a glance toward Caleb, who had finally loaded the colt. "Cover the stairs! Don't let 'em get up there!"

Caleb nodded frantically, handing over the Colt and swinging the rifle toward a side door where another figure loomed. The boy fired, and this time, his shot rang true. The man staggered and dropped to the floor, unmoving.

The gunfire began to ease, replaced by groans and silence. The saloon was choked with smoke and the acrid stench of gunpowder. Bodies littered the floor—Kade's men sprawled among shattered tables, broken glass, and debris. The lantern's flames still flickered at the edge of the wall, casting a ghastly glow over the destruction.

Nash straightened, his chest heaving, sweat streaming down his face. He scanned the saloon, his sharp eyes ensuring no one was left standing. Sadie, breathing hard, pushed her hair back with a trembling hand, her shotgun still gripped tight.

Caleb let out a shaky breath, slumping down behind the table. "Did we—did we get 'em all?"

Nash looked toward the doorway, his eyes cold and calculating. "For now," he muttered. "But this ain't over. Kade'll send more."

Sadie stepped around the bar, her voice raw but steady. "Then we'll be ready for them."

Nash didn't answer. His gaze swept over the carnage, and for the first time, he felt the weight of what they were up against. If Kade wanted Blackrock, he'd burn the whole town to the ground to get it.

And Nash knew the worst was still to come.

The second wave came sooner than even Nash had anticipated. If he'd thought they were at an end he was wrong, and a moment later more of Kade's men launched themselves at the saloon doors.

CHAPTER FOURTEEN

The fight was pure chaos, gunfire thundering through the smoke-choked saloon as Kade's men pushed forward with brutal determination. Nash fired again and again, his Colt kicking hard in his hand. The bodies of Kade's men littered the floor, but more kept coming, forcing their way past the barricade and into the saloon like a relentless tide.

A bullet splintered the wood inches from his head as Nash ducked behind the overturned table, his teeth gritted. He reloaded in a frenzy, sweat streaming down his face, hands slick with grime.

"Caleb, watch yourself!" Nash barked, his voice hoarse.

Caleb had taken up position behind a support beam near the stairs, his rifle braced tight against his shoulder. He squeezed off a shot that dropped one of Kade's men charging in through the doorway, but the recoil knocked him back a step. Before he could recover, a second attacker swung around the corner, pistol raised.

The sharp *crack* of the revolver rang out. Caleb staggered with a strangled cry, his back slamming into the beam as he crumpled to the ground, clutching his shoulder. His rifle clattered away, out of reach.

Wyatt Steele

"Caleb!" Nash shouted, rage lighting his veins. He surged up, firing off two quick shots. One hit the attacker in the gut, the man's scream drowned by the roar of the gunfire. The second round finished him off, sending him sprawling into a heap.

Sadie's shotgun boomed from behind the bar, the sound reverberating off the walls. She caught one man square in the chest as he rushed toward her, the blast sending him sprawling onto his back. Another lunged at her from the side before she could reload, a cruel grin splitting his dirt-streaked face.

Sadie turned, her eyes wide with shock as the man grabbed the shotgun, wrenching it from her hands. She stumbled back, trying to claw for the pistol on her hip, but the attacker was faster, drawing a knife with a sickening hiss of steel.

"Gotcha now, sweetheart," he snarled, advancing on her.

Nash's eyes locked on the scene in an instant. Everything else faded—the gunfire, the smoke, the chaos. With a growl deep in his chest, he sprang over the table, his Colt raised. He fired point-blank, the barrel mere feet from the man's head. The shot roared like a cannon, and the attacker crumpled, the knife clattering harmlessly to the floor as he fell dead at Sadie's feet.

For a moment, everything seemed to stop. Sadie stared at the body, her breath ragged, a streak of blood splattered across her cheek. Her chest heaved, the adrenaline keeping her frozen in place.

Nash grabbed her arm roughly, pulling her upright. "You all right?" he demanded, his voice sharp, his eyes scanning her quickly for any sign of injury.

Sadie swallowed hard, nodding even as her hands trembled. "I—I'm fine," she stammered, her voice cracking.

"Then keep movin'!" Nash ordered, shoving her back toward cover. "We ain't done yet!"

From the corner of his eye, Nash caught movement—another of Kade's men stepping through the smoke, his rifle aimed for Caleb, who was trying to crawl toward his fallen gun, his face pale and strained with pain.

"Stay down, kid!" Nash yelled.

He turned and fired, his shot ripping through the smoke and catching the attacker in the shoulder. The man spun and fell, his rifle discharging harmlessly into the ceiling. Nash didn't wait—he advanced on him, firing again to make sure he stayed down.

More bullets chewed through the walls of the saloon, glass shattering as the windows exploded inward. The air was thick with dust and gunpowder, choking the light. Nash dropped low, holstering his empty Colt and grabbing Caleb's rifle as he passed.

Wyatt Steele

He slid in beside Sadie behind the bar, the wood pockmarked with bullet holes and splinters. Sadie was fumbling with shells, her hands shaking as she reloaded her shotgun. Nash dropped the rifle at her feet, his breath coming hard and fast.

"Get it together," he growled, reloading his revolver. "They ain't stoppin'."

Sadie looked at him, her eyes blazing now with a mixture of terror and fury. She shoved the last shell into her shotgun and snapped it shut. "Neither are we."

Nash nodded once, rising just enough to see over the bar. Through the haze, Kade's men were regrouping near the doorway, more cautious now but still determined to press the attack.

His lip curled in frustration. This wasn't over—not by a long shot. But if they didn't turn the tide soon, there'd be nothing left to defend.

"We hold here," Nash muttered grimly, the Colt ready in his hand. "One way or another."

The gunfire sputtered into uneasy silence, the air thick with smoke and the acrid tang of gunpowder. Nash's chest heaved as he leaned against the bar, reloading his Colt with quick, practiced hands. Across from him, Sadie clutched her shotgun, her knuckles white, her breathing ragged. The saloon creaked under its wounds—shattered glass, splintered wood, the stink of sweat and desperation hanging in the air.

Then a voice rang out, sharp and clear through the chaos.

"NASH!"

The name carried like a whip crack through the smoldering street outside, raw and unmistakable.

Nash froze, his fingers halting as he slid the last bullet into the cylinder. He could hear the slow, measured sound of boots on dirt, punctuated by a mocking drawl.

"It's Kade," gasped Sadie.

"Nash," Kade called again, his voice rising above the stillness. "I know you're in there, hidin' like a rat. You wanna play hero? You wanna save this town? Come out here and face me like a man. Come out, or we'll burn you out."

The words clawed through Nash, stoking the fire that had been building inside him for days. Sadie turned to him, her face pale and streaked with dust, her eyes wide with warning. "Nash... don't."

But Nash didn't look at her. His expression was hard, unreadable, his focus locked somewhere beyond the walls of the saloon. He pushed off the bar, the weight of his guns settling against him like familiar companions.

"He's tryin' to draw you out," Sadie hissed, her voice sharp with desperation. "It's a trap, Nash!"

"Doesn't matter," Nash said quietly, his tone flat but resolute. He snapped the Colt's cylinder shut and holstered it, then checked the Henry rifle slung across his back. Each movement was deliberate, steady, like a man walking toward his fate.

Sadie reached for him, grabbing his arm. "Nash—don't do this. You'll get yourself killed."

He looked at her then, just for a moment, and the fierce concern in her eyes nearly stopped him. "It's been headin' here since the start," he murmured. "Might as well finish it."

She let go, her hand falling away as he turned.

Nash strode toward the saloon doors, the boards groaning beneath his boots. The blood roared in his ears, drowning out everything but the rhythm of his own steps. He passed Caleb slumped against a wall, his face twisted in pain but still conscious enough to watch Nash go. "Nash... you don't gotta—"

"Keep your head down, kid," Nash said without stopping.

The world outside was waiting for him. He pushed through the batwing doors and stepped out onto the street, the sudden burst of light and smoke-soaked air hitting him hard, the flames of burning buildings lit the town with an eerie orange glow.

And there, standing in the middle of the street, was Elijah Kade.

Kade looked almost at ease, his long black duster trailing in the dust as he held his rifle casually across his arm. He was smiling, but there was no warmth in it—just the cruel gleam of a predator who knew he had his prey cornered. His men were scattered, waiting like wolves in the shadows, their guns at the ready.

"There you are," Kade said, his voice dripping with mockery as Nash walked forward. "Took you long enough."

Nash stopped, his shadow stretching long across the dirt. His hand hovered near his Colt, his gaze locked on Kade with cold precision. "You've done enough talkin', Kade."

Kade chuckled low, the sound like gravel. "Is that right? Well, I gotta say, I'm almost impressed, Nash. You've given me more trouble than I expected. But it ends tonight. You hear me?"

Nash didn't flinch. "The only thing endin' tonight is your hold on this town."

Kade's expression twisted, the smile disappearing in a flash. His voice dropped to something darker, deadlier. "You think you're some kind of savior? Some gun-totin' angel come to make things right? You're nothin', Nash. Just another drifter lookin' for a fight he can't win."

Nash's hand twitched at his side, the familiar weight of the Colt calling to him. His mind was a quiet storm, his breath steady despite the tension that hung heavy in the air. Kade took a step forward, his boots scraping the ground, his rifle shifting in his grip.

"You ready, Nash?" Kade growled.

Nash's jaw tightened, his eyes never leaving the man in front of him. "I'm ready."

For a moment, the world seemed to hold its breath. Time slowed, the distant crackle of fire and the faint murmurs of Kade's men the only sounds that broke the silence. Nash could feel his pulse in his ears, steady and sure. This was it.

The heat from the flames clawed at Nash's face as the inferno around him crackled and roared. The street of Blackrock had become a hellscape—smoke rising in black columns, embers floating like dying stars against the dark sky. Kade stood in the center of it, framed by the fire, his long black duster trailing like the wings of some dark omen.

Nash stood twenty paces away, his boots planted firmly in the dirt, the weight of his Colt steady at his side. His face was streaked with sweat and soot, his shirt clinging to him like a second skin. But his eyes—those sharp, cold eyes—stayed fixed on Kade. Unflinching.

Kade tilted his head, a smirk pulling at the corners of his mouth as if this was all just a game, a cruel joke only he was in on. The firelight danced across his face, highlighting the cruel lines etched there by years of power and greed. He rested his hand casually on the rifle slung at his side but didn't yet draw.

"Look at this," Kade sneered, his voice carrying over the chaos like a viper's hiss. "The drifter, standin' tall in the ashes of his own damn mistakes."

Nash didn't move, didn't blink, but the words struck deep, like splinters worming their way beneath his skin.

Kade took a step closer, his boots grinding into the dirt. "I know what kind of man you are, Nash. I've seen your kind before. Washed-up drifters runnin' from their own shadows. Clingin' to dead memories of better days."

Nash's jaw tightened, but he said nothing.

"You think these people see you as a hero?" Kade continued, his voice dripping with mockery. "You ain't no savior. You're a man too scared to die and too broken to live. You're just a damn drifter."

Nash's hand twitched, his fingers flexing near the Colt's worn grip.

The words 'too broken to live,' hit hard. The memory of Emily clawed at something deep inside him, something raw and bitter. His chest ached with it, the way it always did when he remembered her smile, her touch. But he didn't let it show. He couldn't. Not now.

Kade's eyes gleamed as he saw the crack in Nash's composure. "You're just a last chance hero. And you're gunna make these people die to make you one."

The words hit like a hammer to the chest, but Nash stood firm, his breaths slow and steady.

Wyatt Steele

His thumb rested on the hammer of his Colt. He said nothing—there was nothing left to say.

Kade's sneer deepened. "Come on, Nash. Let's see it. Let's see if there's anything left in you worth killin'."

The street fell deathly silent, the air thick with smoke and anticipation. The fire crackled in the ruins, casting flickering shadows that seemed to stretch and dance like ghosts. Nash's mind emptied of everything but this moment. The ache of the past faded, the noise of the fire dimmed, and all he could see was Kade—the man who had terrorized a town, shattered lives, and dug up the ghosts Nash had buried years ago.

Kade's fingers twitched near his rifle. Nash's hand was a blur.

Two shots rang out as one, cracking through the night like a lightning strike.

Kade's smirk froze on his face as the force of the bullet struck him square in the chest. He staggered back, his mouth opening in a stunned, silent gasp. A crimson stain blossomed across his shirt, dark and spreading.

For a moment, he just stood there, as though he couldn't believe it. His eyes locked on Nash one last time, filled with disbelief—and then emptiness.

Kade crumpled to his knees, his hand still gripping the rifle as though he might pull it up again. But the life was already gone from him. He toppled forward into the dirt, his duster pooling around him like a shroud.

Nash lowered his Colt, the smoke curling from the barrel as the echoes of the shots faded into nothing. His chest rose and fell steadily, his expression carved from stone. Around him, the town seemed to hold its breath, the flames still roaring but somehow distant now, muffled by the silence of Kade's death.

Nash stepped forward, his boots heavy against the dirt as he stood over the fallen man. He looked down at Kade's lifeless body, his face illuminated by the glow of the firelight. For all his power, all his threats, Kade looked small now—just another dead man in the dust.

The moment Kade hit the ground, a ripple of panic shot through his men like a lightning strike. One of them shouted something unintelligible—a cry of fear or command, it didn't matter. Their resolve, already wavering, shattered with the fall of their leader. The torches clutched in their hands wavered, and one by one, they began to retreat, turning their horses and spurring them hard into the night.

Nash stood in the center of the street, Colt still hanging loosely at his side, his breathing heavy but controlled. He watched them go, his face carved in exhaustion and grim satisfaction. The battle was over, and Kade's reign of terror had come to an end.

Wyatt Steele

A few gunshots cracked in the darkness, wild and desperate, but there was no organization left, no plan to press forward. Kade's men scattered like dry leaves on the wind, their silhouettes fading into the smoke and gloom, the thunder of hooves receding toward the hills beyond Blackrock.

Caleb's voice broke the silence from somewhere behind him, trembling but steady. "It's over."

Nash didn't answer. He turned slowly, his shoulders sagging just a little as the weight of it all settled in. Kade was dead. The fight was done.

But as he walked back toward the saloon, the flames still burning around him, Nash couldn't shake the feeling that it wasn't over—not for him. It never was.

But Blackrock was broken.

The fires raged on, licking at the charred remains of shops and homes. Smoke rose in thick, black columns into the night sky, blotting out the stars. The acrid stench of burning wood and oil filled the air, settling heavy on the town like a suffocating blanket. Embers drifted and swirled, glowing briefly before vanishing, their light snuffed out like so many lives lost.

Nash turned slowly, taking in the destruction. The saloon's upper windows had been shattered, the front was ripped and splintered by the bullets. The sheriff's office lay dark, its roof caved in where flames had chewed through the rafters. Further down the street, the store was little more than a smoldering husk, its walls collapsed inward.

Figures began to emerge cautiously from doorways and alleyways—townsfolk who had huddled in fear during the fight. Men with soot-streaked faces, women clutching children, eyes wide with disbelief at the ruins around them. The fight was won, but the cost was steep.

Caleb appeared first, one arm cradled against his bloodied shoulder as he limped toward Nash. His face was pale but resolute, his gaze flicking between Nash and Kade's motionless body. "They're gone," he rasped, his voice barely above a whisper. "They're really gone."

Nash nodded, holstering his Colt with deliberate care.

Caleb exhaled shakily, his voice hoarse. "It's done."

Nash looked away, his gaze sweeping the town again. "Yeah," he said softly. "It's done."

But the words rang hollow. The echoes of gunfire still lingered in his ears, drowned only by the roar of the flames eating what little remained of Blackrock's stubborn pride. The street that had been alive with violence moments ago was now eerily quiet, save for the groans of wood collapsing and the low cries of those gathering the wounded.

With a weary sigh, Nash turned and walked toward the saloon, his silhouette dark against the glow of the dying fires. Some of Blackrock was still standing, and for now, that would have to be enough.

Nash made his way up the saloon steps, stepping over shattered glass and broken furniture. The saloon had been battered in the fight—the balcony railing splintered, windows blown out, bullet holes riddling the walls—but it still stood. And so did Sadie.

Nash stepped through the splintered saloon doors, the weight of the long night hanging on his shoulders. The air inside was thick with smoke and dust, faint traces of gunpowder still lingering like ghosts. He moved quietly, his boots thudding against the scuffed wooden floor as he set the Henry rifle down on the bar with a heavy thud.

Sadie stood behind it, her face streaked with soot, hair wild and falling around her face, the shotgun still clutched in her hands like she wasn't sure if the fight was really over. She looked at him, her eyes meeting his—wide, raw, and full of everything she hadn't said. For a moment, neither of them moved. The only sound was the faint creak of the saloon settling, the quiet after the storm.

Nash didn't say a word. He just stepped forward, his gaze locked on hers. His fingers curled around the barrel of her shotgun, gently prying it from her hands as her grip weakened.

Revenge of the Gunfighter

The weapon clattered softly as he laid it next to the Henry, forgotten.

And then, without hesitation, he pulled her to him.

Sadie crashed against his chest, her hands grabbing for his shirt as though she were afraid he'd slip away. Nash's arms wrapped around her, fierce and unyielding, his hold a mix of desperation and relief. He tilted her chin up, and the moment their lips met, the world outside ceased to exist.

The kiss was hot, urgent—raw in a way that only two people who had nearly lost everything could understand. Sadie melted into him, her need as great as his. She pressed closer, fingers tangling in his shirt as though trying to pull him deeper into her. Nash's hand slid up her back, his calloused fingers finding the curve of her neck, holding her there as he kissed her with the kind of hunger that couldn't be denied.

There was nothing soft about it—no hesitation, no second-guessing. It was the kiss of two people who'd walked through fire, both of them scorched but still standing. Nash could feel her trembling against him, but whether it was from exhaustion, relief, or the force of her own need, he didn't know. And he didn't care. He kissed her harder, like he could steal her breath and give her his in return.

Finally, they broke apart, both of them gasping, foreheads pressed together. Nash's eyes searched hers, dark and conflicted, as if he was still trying to convince himself this was real—that it was okay to want this.

Sadie's voice came soft, her breath brushing against his lips. "Don't go thinking you're done here, cowboy."

Nash exhaled sharply, a ghost of a smile tugging at the corners of his mouth. "Wouldn't dream of it."

Behind them the batwing doors creaked, the sound cutting through the silence like a knife. Sheriff Amos stepped inside, his boots scuffing against the floorboards. He stopped just short of the bar, his eyes scanning the room, taking in the wreckage and the bodies outside visible through the shattered windows.

"Looks like you did okay," Amos drawled, his voice casual, but his gaze was wary as it settled on Nash.

Nash turned slowly, his body tensing. He said nothing at first, letting the weight of Amos's words hang in the air. His eyes narrowed, cold and calculating as they locked onto the sheriff. Sadie stepped back instinctively, sensing the shift in the room.

"You were there," Nash said finally, his voice low and measured. He didn't move, but every muscle in his body was coiled. "The night Jenkins bought me that drink. You were sittin' in the corner, listenin'. You knew."

Amos stiffened, his face shifting from nonchalance to guarded defensiveness. "Knew what?" he asked, though his voice lacked conviction.

Nash tilted his head slightly, his jaw tightening. "Don't play dumb with me. You told Kade that Jankin's had been fool enough to buy me a whiskey, And Kade knew my name. The only way he could've known is if someone told him. Someone who was supposed to protect this town."

Amos's face paled, but his pride wouldn't let him back down. "You've got no proof," he said, his voice growing harsher. "You think you're some kind of saint, Nash? Coming in here, stirring up trouble. You don't know how hard it's been—"

"One word," Nash interrupted, his voice cutting through Amos's excuses like a whip. "Traitor."

Amos's eyes flickered with panic, realizing too late that Nash wasn't just guessing—he knew. His hand twitched toward his gun, a foolish move made in desperation. But Nash had been watching for it. Before Amos could even clear the holster, Nash's hand moved like lightning, pulling the Perry single-shot pistol from his jacket.

The crack of the gun echoed through the saloon, sharp and final. Amos staggered back, his face frozen in shock as his hand dropped from his holster. He clutched at his chest, his fingers brushing the tin star pinned there, now punched clean through by Nash's bullet. He collapsed onto the floor, the star glinting faintly in the dim light.

For a moment, the saloon was silent again, save for the sound of Amos's body hitting the floorboards. Sadie's breath hitched, her wide eyes darting between Nash and the fallen sheriff.

Nash exhaled, the tension in his shoulders easing slightly. He turned back to Sadie, holstering the Perry with a fluid motion. His hands found her waist, pulling her close again as if nothing had happened. Sadie let out a shaky breath but didn't resist, her arms slipping around him.

"If anyone's lookin'," Nash murmured, his voice low and rough, "they'll see he was shot clean through the center of that star. Seems fitting."

Sadie's lips curved into a faint smile, despite the lingering adrenaline in her veins. "You've got a hell of a way of makin' a statement, cowboy."

Nash chuckled softly, leaning down to kiss her again. The warmth of her lips against his dulled the weight of what had just happened, if only for a moment. Outside, the first light of dawn began creeping into the sky, casting long shadows over the quiet town of Blackrock. It was over—for now. For the moment, though, he held Sadie tighter, as if daring the world to try.

Revenge of the Gunfighter

Her arms stayed wrapped around him, and for the first time in a long while, Nash let himself believe there might be something more than the trail waiting for him—something worth staying for.

Wyatt Steele

EPILOGUE

The room was still and warm, the soft glow of the lantern casting amber light over the walls. Nash lay on his back, his body sprawled lazily across the bed, his chest rising and falling with deep, steady breaths. A light sheen of sweat on his skin caught the low light. He looked content—a rare sight on a man whose face often wore the shadow of trouble.

Sadie rested against him, her head tucked into the crook of his shoulder, one arm draped loosely across his chest. She traced idle patterns against his skin with her fingertips, slow and absent, as if savoring the quiet moment as much as he was. The sheets were tangled at their waists, and the faint scent of whiskey and lavender lingered in the air.

For once, Nash felt a rare, unfamiliar kind of peace. He turned his head slightly, watching Sadie, her auburn hair spilling over his shoulder in a curtain of soft waves. He let out a low hum of satisfaction and let his fingers slide through her hair, his touch gentle.

A thought had been nagging at him for a while now—something about her, something unspoken—and for the first time, he let himself ask.

"Sadie..." he murmured, his voice a low, gravelly drawl. "Tell me about your husband."

Sadie didn't stop tracing her fingers across his chest, but her body stiffened just slightly. For a beat, she said nothing, as though considering what to say—or how much.

"His name's Albert," she said at last, her voice soft but clear.

Nash frowned faintly, shifting next to her. She hadn't said *was*. She'd said *is*. His mind caught on that word like a burr snagging wool. He pulled his head back a little, looking down at her. "Albert?"

Sadie turned her face up toward him, a teasing glint in her eye. "That's his name. Albert Macallister."

Nash's brow furrowed. "*Was* his name?" he pressed carefully. "You talk like he's still kickin'."

Sadie let out a low laugh, one full of amusement, and slid her hand up to rest under her chin as she gazed at him. "Far as I know, he is."

The room seemed to still. Nash shifted, his contentment cracking as he pushed himself up slightly, sliding her arm off his chest. "I thought your husband was *dead,* Sadie."

She laughed again, a sound that seemed to only make Nash's frown deepen. "Well, that's where *thought* got you, Cowboy," she teased, propping herself up on one elbow. "No turnin' back now."

Wyatt Steele

Nash stared at her for a moment, half incredulous, half annoyed. "Damn it, Sadie," he muttered, scrubbing a hand through his damp hair. "I didn't think I was takin' a *wed woman* to my bed."

Sadie's lips curled into an amused smile, but there was something softer behind her eyes. "Don't get your feathers ruffled. I haven't been anyone's wife in a long time. Not really."

"That supposed to make me feel better?" Nash muttered, though there wasn't as much bite in his voice as he intended.

Sadie sat up fully, pulling the sheet around herself as she turned to face him, her tone more measured now. "Albert worked for the railway. Good money, back then. Trouble was, he'd be gone for weeks. Sometimes months." She shrugged, though her gaze drifted to the floor, thoughtful. "Then one day, he just didn't come back."

Nash's gaze softened slightly, but he didn't say anything, letting her go on.

"I grieved for him, Nash. Spent a year thinkin' he was dead. Mourned him proper, too." She glanced at him with a wry smile. "Then, two years after he left, word came through that Albert was holed up in Mintoville with a woman half his age."

Nash's jaw worked silently as he took that in.

Sadie shook her head, her voice light but edged with an old bitterness. "For a while, I was mad as hell. I wanted to track him down, drag him back by his boots, and throw him in a pig trough. But then I let it go."

"You just... let it go?" Nash asked, his brow lifting.

Sadie nodded. "What was the point holdin' on to it? I inherited this saloon from my pa, and I found I liked runnin' it on my own. Liked bein' my own boss, makin' my own rules. Life with Albert had been good while it lasted, sure. But we were so rarely together it was always like bein' newlyweds—always hungry for each other, always fresh."

Nash couldn't hide his surprise. "That's a hell of a marriage."

Sadie laughed, a small, genuine sound. "Maybe. But I saw what happened to other folks—livin' side by side every day, growin' tired, fightin'. Albert and I didn't have time for that." She turned to him then, meeting his gaze squarely. "That's why I won't hold you here, Nash. But you're welcome back, once in while."

He stared at her, her words settling in his chest like a stone thrown into a still pond, the ripples spreading.

She leaned in closer, her voice dropping into a teasing whisper. "Maybe *twice* in a while."

The corner of Nash's mouth tugged upward despite himself, his defenses cracking. He shook his head slowly, his low voice rumbling, "Only twice, huh?"

Sadie smiled mischievously. "Maybe three times in a while."

Nash rolled on top of her, pinning her to the bed. "Three times in a while?" he murmured, his voice softer now, that familiar spark of trouble in his eyes, as he felt desire rising within him again.

"I could live with that," she whispered, tilting her chin up.

Nash didn't fight it anymore. He leaned down, drawing her closer, kissing her, slow and deep, letting the moment pull him in. Her arms slipped around his neck, holding him there like she'd been waiting for it.

For just a little while longer, the world outside didn't exist. There was no Kade, no Blackrock, no past that haunted him. Just her. Just now.

And though Nash would never say it aloud, the thought lingered in the back of his mind as he kissed her. *Maybe three times in a while was something worth holding onto.*

Revenge of the Gunfighter

Next Book in this series – The Wrath of the Gunfighter

Why not ride with Wyatt Earp? Available in Large Print. *Vendetta Ride*, written by Wyatt Steele, is a hard-hitting western based on real history and the real men who carved their names into it with lead.

Follow **Wyatt Earp and Doc Holliday** as they step beyond the law and into legend—tracking the killers of Morgan Earp across the ruthless frontier of Arizona Territory.

It's sharp, it's brutal, and it's grounded in truth. These men lived. These events happened. What follows is their reckoning.

So while Nash reloads for his next trail, saddle up with *Vendetta Ride.*
Justice rides faster with a six-gun.
"Gritty, gripping, and steeped in history—Wyatt Steele brings the West to life like never before."

Looking for more grit, dust, and justice served from the barrel of a gun?

Meet Ryder – Also by Wyatt Steele. He rides alone. Built like a thundercloud and twice as hard to move. No badge. No allegiance. Just a Colt on his hip, a past that won't stay buried, and a code he keeps sharper than his knife.

Wyatt Steele

If you like your Westerns lean, brutal, and unforgiving—<u>**the Ryder series**</u> delivers. Blood-soaked trails, buried secrets, and men who'd rather shoot than speak. Start with <u>***Ryder – Gone to Hell***</u> and ride straight into a story where no one's innocent, and survival comes at a price.

Because while Nash fights for justice… **Ryder fights to stay one step ahead of hell.** Readers are calling it "gritty, gripping, and impossible to put down!"

ALSO BY WYATT STEELE

<u>TRAIL OF THE GUNFIGHTER SERIES</u>

<u>VENDETTA RIDE – THE WRATH OF WYATT EARP</u>

<u>THE OUTLAW McCOY SERIES</u>

<u>RYDER WESTERN SERIES</u>

<u>DRIFTER GRITTY WESTERN SERIES</u>

Printed in Dunstable, United Kingdom